Sail Away

Noël Coward

A Samuel French Acting Edition

FOUNDED 1830

SAMUELFRENCH.COM
SAMUELFRENCH-LONDON.CO.UK

ISBN 978-0-573-69754-8

www.SamuelFrench.com
www.SamuelFrench-London.co.uk

FOR PRODUCTION ENQUIRIES

UNITED STATES AND CANADA
Info@SamuelFrench.com
1-866-598-8449

Each title is subject to availability from Samuel French, depending upon country of performance. Please be aware that *SAIL AWAY* may not be licensed by Samuel French in your territory. Professional and amateur producers should contact the nearest Samuel French office or licensing partner to verify availability.

MUSIC USE NOTE

Licensees are solely responsible for obtaining formal written permission from copyright owners to use copyrighted music in the performance of this play and are strongly cautioned to do so. If no such permission is obtained by the licensee, then the licensee must use only original music that the licensee owns and controls. Licensees are solely responsible and liable for all music clearances and shall indemnify the copyright owners of the play(s) and their licensing agent, Samuel French, against any costs, expenses, losses and liabilities arising from the use of music by licensees. Please contact the appropriate music licensing authority in your territory for the rights to any incidental music.

IMPORTANT BILLING AND CREDIT REQUIREMENTS

If you have obtained performance rights to this title, please refer to your licensing agreement for important billing and credit requirements.

SAIL AWAY was first presented by Bonard Productions in association with Charles Russell at the Colonial Theatre in Boston on August 9, 1961. The company moved to the Forrest Theatre in Philadelphia on September 7. The production was subsequently presented at the Broadhurst Theatre in New York City on October 3, 1961. The Broadhurst performance was directed by Noël Coward, with sets by Oliver Smith, costumes by Helene Pons and Oliver Smith, lights by Peggy Clark, and choreography by Joe Layton. The cast was as follows:

JOE. . . . . Charles Braswell

SHUTTLEWORTH . . . . Keith Prentice

RAWLINGS . . . . James Pritchett

SIR GERARD NUTFIELD . . . . .C. Stafford Dickens

LADY NUTFIELD . . . . Margaret Mower

BARNABY SLADE . . . . .Grover Dale

ELMER CANDIJACK. . . . . Henry Lawrence

MAIMIE CANDIJACK . . . . Betty Jane Watsons

GLEN CANDIJACK. . . . . Alan Helms

SHIRLEY CANDIJACK . . . . .Patti Mariano

MR. SWEENEY . . . . .C. Stafford Dickens

MRS. SWEENEY . . . . Paula Bauersmith

ELINOR SPENCER-BOLLARD. . . . . .Alice Pearce

NANCY FOYLE . . . . Patricia Harty

ALVIN LUSH. . . . . .Paul O'Keefe

MRS. LUSH. . . . . Evelyn Russell

JOHN VAN MIER . . . . .James Hurst

MRS. VAN MIER . . . . Margalo Gillmore

MIMI PARAGON. . . . . .Elaine Stritch

DECK STEWARD. . . . . .James Frashers

ALI . Charles Braswell

MAN FROM AMERICAN EXPRESS . . . . Richard Woods

LITTLE ONES. . . . . Bobby Allen, Paul Gross,
        Bridget Knapp, Mary Ellen O'Keefe, Dennis Scott, Christopher Votos

GIRL PASSENGER . . . . .Ann Fraser

EXTRAS. . . . . Jere Admire, Don Atkinson, Gary Crabbe, David Evans,
        Pat Ferier, Dorothy Frank, James Frasher, Gene Gavin, Curtis
        Hood,Wish Mary Hunt, Cheryl Kilgreen, Nancy Lynch, Patti
        Mariano, Allan Peterson, Alice Shanahan, Dan Siretta, Gloria Stevens

SAIL AWAY had its London premiere at the Savoy Theatre on June 21, 1961.

In November of 1999, Elaine Stritch played Mimi in two weeks of concert performances at Carnegie Hall's Weill Recital Hall. The concert was directed by Gerald Gutierrez.

CHARACTERS

MIMI PARAGON

JOHNNY VAN MIER

MRS. VAN MIER

BARNABY SLADE

NANCY FOYLE

ELINOR SPENCER BOLLARD

SIR GERARD NUTFIELD

LADY NUTFIELD

MR. SWEENEY

MRS. SWEENEY

JOE THE PURSER

MRS. LUSH

ALVIN LUSH

MR. ELMER CANDIJACK

MRS. MAMIE CANDIJACK

MR. RAWLINGS

SHUTTLEWORTH

SCENE LIST

ACT ONE

ACT TWO

SONG LIST

ACT ONE

Scene 1	'Come to Me'	**MIMI PARAGON** and **STEWARDS**
2	'Sail Away'	**JOHNNY VAN MIER**
	'Come to Me' Reprise	**MIMI PARAGON**
3	'Where Shall I Find Him'	**NANCY**
4	'Beatnik Love Affair'	**BARNABY**
	'Later Than Spring'	**JOHNNY**
	'The Customer's Always Right'	**JOE** and **STEWARDS**
5	'Useless Useful Phrases'	**MIMI**
6	'Where Shall I Find Her' Reprise	**BARNABY**
7	'The Little Ones' ABC'	**MIMI** and **CHILDREN**
8	'Go Slow Johnny'	**JOHNNY**
9	'You're a Long Long Way from America'	**MIMI** and **COMPANY**

ACT TWO

Scene 1	'The Customer's Always Right'	**ALI** and **ARABS**
	'Something's Very Strange	**MIMI**
2	'Italian Wedding Ballet'	
3	'Don't Turn Away from Love'	**JOHNNY**
4	'When You Want Me'	**NANCY** and **BARNABY**
5	'Bronxville Darby & Joan'	**MR.** and **MRS. SWEENEY**
6	'Later Than Spring' Reprise	**MIMI**
7	'When You Want Me' Reprise	**COMPANY**
	'Why Do the Wrong People Travel'	**MIMI**

HOW *SAIL AWAY* SAILED AWAY

In early 1956, Noël Coward was in Jamaica and planning a new project. He would write a film script – "a brittle, stylised, sophisticated, insignificant comedy with music to be called *Later Than Spring... It will be as unexpected as Cosi Fan Tutte.*" And he felt it would be a perfect vehicle for Marlene Dietrich and himself.

Two years later, the film – as well as Mozart and Marlene – had been set aside and he was working on a musical about Mrs. Wentworth-Brewster (the lady who found late life love in *A Bar on the Piccola Marina*).

"Of course, she will have to shed a few years and a few pounds, since she is to be played by Ethel Merman on a cruise. She will naturally [be] glamourised and also 'Americanised'."

Merman didn't see herself in the part. Nor did Rosalind Russell, nor did Judy Holliday. Not surprisingly, perhaps, very few 'mature' Broadway leading ladies had ever wanted to play the ugly duckling, even when they knew a swan was waiting in the wings.

By December 1960 – "I have decided to change the title to *Sail Away,* which is a gayer title and more appropriate. I wrote yesterday a wonderful opening number for Kay Thompson..."

But Ms.Thompson didn't fancy an ocean voyage either, so Mrs. Wentworth-Brewster was again cheated of her reincarnatory cruise. Which left Noël with a first act and a handful of songs.

He decided that the reason he couldn't cast the main role was that she was essentially unattractive. The surgeon in him surfaced. The leading characters would have to go. "They are not real and never were... they are hangovers from that abortive enterprise and have been worrying me ever since."

The setting switched to a British cruise liner, the S.S.CORONIA but the drama of actually constructing the show was only just beginning...

By the time it opened in Boston on August 9, 1961, the leading characters were Verity Craig (played by opera star Jean Fenn), an unhappy wife leaving her husband behind and contemplating divorce and even suicide, and Johnny Van Mier, another passenger she finds herself attracted to. Their romance was to provide "the tender, lyrical moments."

Boston audiences didn't share that feeling. The couple sang their numbers well enough but the dialogue Noel had given them was beyond them. Subconsciously, perhaps, he had written what could only be performed by Noel & Gertie.

---

* All quotations are by Noël Coward and were sourced from his personal letters and diaries.

In Philadelphia...the same audience reaction. The main story was downbeat and depressing.

Out came the surgeon's knife. Out went the main plot. Up with the sub-plot.

Mimi Paragon, the cruise director (Elaine Stritch), hitherto the comedy interest, would now be the subject of Johnny's affections and Mimi would now become the comedic *and* romantic lead.

Noel had first become impressed by 'Stritchie' in a 1958 musical called *Goldilocks*. She had, he found, something of an Ethel Merman quality: a combination of the streetwise and the soft-hearted.

And "anyone who can dance with a 10-foot bear is my kind of performer."

Sail Away docked at the Broadhurst Theatre, New York on October 3, 1961, and Elaine Stritch became an overnight star. The show itself ran for 167 performances and Stritchie then took the production to London's Savoy Theatre the following year. In 1999 – Noel's centenary year – she reprised the role for two weeks of concert performances at Carnegie Hall.

The personal rapport between her and Noel lasted for the rest of both of their lives. A letter from Noel to his star only a few days after the Broadway opening gives something of the flavour...

Darling Stritchie,

I hope that you are well; that your cold is better, that you are singing divinely; that you are putting on weight; that you are not belting too much; that your skin is clear and free from spots and other blemishes; that you are delivering my brilliant material in the manner in which it SHOULD be delivered; that you are not making too many God-damned suggestions; that your breath is relatively free from the sinful taint of alcohol; that you are going regularly to confession and everywhere else that is necessary to go regularly. I also hope that you are not encouraging those dear little doggies to behave in such a fashion on the stage that they bring disrepute to the fair name of Equity and add fuel to the already prevalent suspicion that our gallant little company is not, by and large, entirely normal; that you are not taking those silly Walter Kerrs and Agnes B. De Mille to the Pavillon for lunch every day. They only exhaust you and drain your energy and however much you want to keep in with them, you must remember that your first duty is to me and the Catholic Church - in that order.

I remain yours sincerely with mad hot kisses.

And until she sailed away herself at the age of 88, Stritchie returned them.

– Barry Day

ACT ONE

[MUSIC #1: "OVERTURE"]

[MUSIC #2: "OPENING SHIP MUSIC"]

(The dock at night. The ship is in the background with all the portholes lighted. At the entrance to the boarding gangway neatly uniformed stewards are waiting to escort the **PASSENGERS**.)

(As the scene begins, the opening music starts and there is a great deal of general movement and hurrying about as sailing time draws near. Singly and in groups, the **PASSENGERS** arrive. First is a **WOMAN PASSENGER** and a **LITTLE GIRL**. The **WOMAN** hands her luggage and the **LITTLE GIRL** to a **STEWARD** who passes the luggage and the **CHILD** very efficiently down a long line of **STEWARDS** that has formed at the gangway. **ANOTHER WOMAN** enters with a **LITTLE GIRL** and her luggage and **CHILD** are passed from **STEWARD** to **STEWARD**.)

(**SIR GERARD** and **LADY NUTFIELD** come on. He is tall and distinguished and is an ex-British Colonial Governor, so exquisitely true to form that he wears a monocle. **LADY NUTFIELD** is pale and wispy and has obviously been exposed far too long to tropic suns.)

(**MR. RAWLINGS**, a gentleman who drinks too much, staggers aboard and makes his way to the **PURSER**.)

(**BARNABY SLADE**, an eager young man with his ticket in his mouth, emerges from the gangway as though he had been propelled from a gun. He is laden with cameras, a pile of books tied up with string and several packages. **ELMER** and **MAIMIE** are young middle-aged. Their son *and daughter,* **GLEN** *and* **SHIRLEY**, *are in their late teens or early twenties.* **ALL FOUR** *of them are noisy, slightly common and filled with good will. Chattering like magpies they are led off to their cabin.)*

*(***JOHN VAN MIER**, *a tall handsome young man in his twenties, comes on accompanied by his mother,* **MRS. VAN MIER**, *a faded once pretty woman with a steely eye and the authoritative air of a prominent Bostonian matron.* **JOE** *crosses to meet her.)*

*(***MR. & MRS. SWEENEY** *appear from the gangway.* **THEY** *are an elderly couple. She wears a large mauve orchid attached to the collar of her suit which tickles her chin. She smiles at everyone with overpowering sweetness as she and her* **HUSBAND** *are led away.)*

*(***NANCY FOYLE**, *a simply dressed, pretty young girl, comes on with her aunt,* **MRS. SPENCER BOLLARD**. **ELINOR SPENCER BOLLARD** *is a famous American novelist. She is a well-disposed megalomaniac and the ideal of women's clubs from San Francisco to Portland, Maine. As they start to cross the stage, an* **AUTOGRAPH HUNTER** *rushes on and presents her book to* **ELINOR**. *She graciously signs it as* **BARNABY** *leaps forward to snap a picture of the smiling* **NANCY**.)*

*(***ALVIN LUSH** *races onto the stage. He is about ten years old and obviously an impossible child. His mother,* **MRS. LUSH**, *is right behind him. She is a sharp woman with overdone hair.* **ALVIN** *runs past the line of* **STEWARDS** *knocking the luggage out of their hands.)*

(By the time **ALL THESE CHARACTERS** *have made their entrances the general hubbub has abated slightly. As the* **PASSENGERS** *exit up the stairs and off, the music comes to an end.)*

SHUTTLEWORTH. She's late.

JOE. Mimi's always late. She's a last minute girl don't woffy it's still half an hour before sailing time.

SHUTTLEWORTH. Oh, Carrington, pop down and see if you can find Mrs. Paragon.

CARRINGTON. Righto.

(**MIMI** *enters with* **ADLAI** *and a large flowering plant.*)

CARRINGTON. Mimi.

MIMI. Sweet God I've made it…

JOE. Only just.

MIMI. Don't look disapproving, Joe darling. It will make deep furrows down your lovely sunburned cheeks and sad, defeated bags under your eyes. What sort of an assignment have we got this trip? Any drunks, junkies or ladies of light reputation?

JOE. It's too early to tell yet.

BREWSTER. Mimi!

MIMI. Brewster, be an angel right from heaven and take Adlai to the tip topmost deck and give him a tiny walk. He's over excited and hasn't had a moment. Be the best boy, Adlai.

JOE. Now you know he ought to go straight to the kennels.

MIMI. Nonsense, dear, we've been through all that before. If Adlai sleeps in the kennel I sleep in the kennel and that would be death to prestige. If you are forbidding, unapproachable, and uncooperative, Joe darling, mother will lock herself in her divine inside cabin and you'll have to run those damned Bingo tournaments on your own. Put that in my room will you?

JOE. Now see here Mimi

MIMI. How glorious to be home again after those dreary sun drenched days on West Seventy-Third street. Boys you look wonderful.

STEWARDS. So do you, Mimi!

(*applause*)

MIMI. That's the sort of welcome that warms my old heart… makes me feel like Queen Victoria.

(**STEWARDS** *bring* **MIMI** *'s luggage, a rocking chair, and balloons.*)

[MUSIC #3: "COME TO ME"]

STEWARDS. *(singing)*
> THANK THE LORD
> MIMI PARAGON'S ON BOARD
> SHE CAN ORGANIZE THE HORDE
> OF MORONS – WE SAID MORONS
> THAT WE TAKE ABOARD
> SHE WILL SEE THAT THEY'RE OCCUPIED EVERY MOMENT OF
>   THE DAY
> KEEP THE FATHEADS OUT OF OUR WAY
> HURRAY HURRAY HURRAY!
> GIVE A CHEER
> MIMI PARAGON IS HERE
> SHE WILL FIRMLY COMMANDEER
> THE DUMB-CLUCKS – WE SAID DUMB-CLUCKS
> TILL THEY'RE ON THEIR EAR
> SHE WILL RIDE 'EM TILL THEY QUALIFY FOR THE
>   PSYCHOPATHIC WARD
> HALLELUJAH – THANK THE LORD
> MIMI PARAGON'S ON BOARD

MIMI.
> THEY CHRISTENED ME MIMI
> WHICH MAY APPEAR AFFECTED
> BUT HEAVEN FORBID THAT I SHOULD SHIRK
> THE WORK THAT I'VE SELECTED
> TO BE A PROFESSIONAL PEPPER-UPPER
> ISN'T EVERYONE'S CUPPA TEA
> BUT I'VE WIT AND GUILE
> AND A BIG FALSE SMILE
> AND THE TOURISTS RELY ON ME.

BOYS.
> THAT'S QUITE, QUITE TRUE
> THEY ALWAYS DO
> THEY'RE CRAZY ABOUT MIMI.

MIMI.

ON THE VERY FIRST DREADFUL DAY
I STAND THEM IN LINE

BOYS.

SHE STANDS THEM IN LINE

MIMI.

I KEEP THEM IN LINE

BOYS.

SHE KEEPS THEM IN LINE

MIMI.

I STAND THEM IN LINE AND SAY
IF YOU'RE MAD KEEN TO BE CULTURAL
I'M THE GAL
WITH WHOM YOU SHOULD ROAM
I CAN SHOW YOU EVERY RUIN FROM JERUSALEM TO GREECE
ALSO QUITE A FEW BETWEEN ANTIBES AND NICE
IF YOU CAN'T LIVE WITHOUT ANTIQUE POTS
I'LL FIND LOTS FOR YOU TO TAKE HOME
IF YOU LONG TO TAKE BAD PHOTOGRAPHS OF CLASSICAL
    DEBRIS
COME TO ME – COME TO ME
IF YOU WANT TO CROUCH IN CHURCHES TILL YOU'VE
    WATER ON THE KNEE
COME TO ME POOR FOOLS – COME TO ME.

BOYS.

SHE'S TERRIBLY ENERGETIC
SHE'S SO FULL OF VIM AND ZIP
IF WE HIT A GALE
AND THE TURBINES FAIL
SHE CAN EASILY DRIVE THE SHIP

MIMI.

AND IF TO PLAY GAMES IS WHAT YOU CALL FUN
I'M THE ONE
TO KEEP YOU IN FORM
I CAN ORGANIZE A TREASURE HUNT OR EVEN CLOCKWORK
    TRAINS
ANYTHING TO OCCUPY THEIR POOR DIM BRAINS.
WE'VE SOME FINE BACKGAMMON BOARDS ON BOARD

IF THE LORD SHOULD SEND US A STORM
IF CANASTA BRIDGE OR BINGO ARE YOUR KIND OF
    JAMBOREE
COME TO ME – COME TO ME
BUT IF YOU WANT TO PLAY STRIP POKER WITH THE GIRLS
    IN CABIN B
COME TO ME – DEAR BOYS – COME TO ME – DEAR BOYS

MIMI. *(spoken)* We will now have one fast chorus of 'Beyond the Blue Horizon.'

(Resume singing)

COME TO ME!

[MUSIC #3A: "COME TO ME – UTILITY"]

Scene Two

(THE SUN DECK)

(The previous scene dissolves to the Sun Deck as the music "Sail Away" continues. The rails are lined with **PASSENGERS** *all shouting and talking at once. There is a blast from the ship's siren and it is obvious that the ship is beginning to move slowly out into the Hudson River.)*

*(***SIR GERARD*** and *****LADY NUTFIELD*** and *****MRS. LUSH*** and *****ALVIN*** are at the rail Downstage Right. The* **CANDIJACK FAMILY** *Downstage Left are hanging over the rail and shrieking with excitement.)*

MR. CANDIJACK. I can still see Aunt Trudi.

GLEN. Where – where?

MR. CANDIJACK. There. Just behind the woman in the red hat. Hi, Aunt Trudi. *(shouting)* Don't forget to get the cat fixed. You'll never have any peace until you do.

MRS. CANDIJACK. Oh, Elmer!

MRS. LUSH. Keep still Alvin. You don't want to fall in the water do you?

ALVIN. I'm a seagull…I'm a seagull.

MRS. LUSH. Yes dear, you're a great big gorgeous seagull.

(There is the blast of the ship's siren. **ALVIN** *blows his whistle.)*

SIR GERARD. Is it quite necessary for your little boy to go on blowing that whistle? There's quite enough noise as it is.

MRS. LUSH. The child's only enjoying himself, Give mother that whistle Alvin you're upsetting this poor old gentleman. *(She takes the whistle and blows it defiantly.)* I'm enjoying myself too.

(She goes off with **ALVIN***.)*

SIR GERARD. These Americans! Savages every one of them –
Savages!

(**MRS. VAN MIER** *moves to the lower rail when the*
CANDIJACK FAMILY *have left it.*)

JOHNNY. Mother, don't let's go on about it any more. You
were right and I was wrong. Let's leave it at that

MRS. MIER. I knew she was no good the first moment I set
eyes on her.

JOHNNY. Nonsense, mother. You liked her very much, so
did everybody else.

MRS. MIER. She had a hard mouth dear, and a calculating
expression. Of course you were too besotted about her
to notice.

JOHNNY. I wasn't particularly besotted about her then. It
was later that I fell in love with her.

MRS. MIER. Are you still?

JOHNNY. Still what?

MRS. MIER. In love with her?

JOHNNY. One can't stop being in love all in a minute. I'm
doing my best.

MRS. MIER. I can't bear you to be unhappy Johnny. You're
all I've got you know.

JOHNNY. Yes mother of course I know. But you mustn't
woffy about me so much. I'll be alright I promise I will.

MRS. MIER. I know you're secretly blaming me for all this.

JOHNNY. I'm not blaming anyone except myself.

MRS. MIER. I know you've resented some of the things I've
said.

JOHNNY. Oh mother.

MRS. MIER. It's no use denying it. A mother's instincts are
seldom wrong.

JOHNNY. A mother's instincts are very often wrong when
she starts meddling with her son's love affairs.

MRS. MIER. You see I was right. You do blame me.

JOHNNY. Once and for all mother will you stop going on like this.

MRS. MIER. There's no need to shout dear.

JOHNNY. Now listen mother. We're setting off on this cruise together you for my sake; me, for your sake. I'm to get over my troubles while you forget about being ill and get well and strong again. Let's for God's sake start off on the right foot. Now just be a dear and go to your cabin and help your stewardess to unpack. I don't want to talk any more.

MRS. MIER. You certainly do remind me or your poor father sometimes.

(She exits.)

JOHNNY. Goddamn it…damn everything!

[MUSIC #4: "SAIL AWAY"]

(singing)

A DIFFERENT SKY
NEW WORLDS TO GAZE UPON
THE STRANGE EXCITEMENT OR AN UNFAMILIAR SHORE

ONE MORE GOODBYE
ONE MORE ILLUSION GONE
JUST CUT YOUR LOSSES
AND BEGIN ONCE MORE.

WHEN THE STORM CLOUDS ARE RIDING THROUGH A
    WINTER SKY
SAIL AWAY – SAIL AWAY
WHEN THE LOVE-LIGHT IS FADING IN YOUR SWEETHEART'S
    EYE
SAIL AWAY – SAIL AWAY
WHEN YOU FEEL YOUR SONG IS ORCHESTRATED WRONG
WHY SHOULD YOU PROLONG
YOUR STAY?
WHEN THE WIND AND THE WEATHER BLOW YOUR DREAMS
    SKY HIGH
SAIL AWAY – SAIL AWAY – SAIL AWAY!

*(At the end of **JOHNNY**'s verse and refrain of "Sail Away" the lights which have dimmed a little come up again, **PASSENGERS** walk back and forth. The **NUTFIELDS** reappear and are accosted by **MRS. VAN MIER. JOHNNY** disappears temporarily among the other **PASSENGERS**.)*

MRS. MIER. Sir Gerard! What a pleasant surprise. I had no idea you were on board. I am Mrs. Van Mier. We met in Washington with the dear Cunninghams. Don't you remember?

SIR GERARD. Ah, yes…of course.

MRS. MIER. I had a letter from Hester Cunningham only last week. Her eldest girl is getting married at last

SIR GERARD. Is that the noisy one or the quiet one?

MRS. MIER. Oh, the quiet one. The noisy one became a nun.

*(**MIMI** enters from up left.)*

MIMI. Welcome aboard, Mrs. Van Mier…how do you do? And you are Sir Gerard Nutfield?

SIR GERARD. That is correct.

MIMI. I knew it…just from the way you were standing I knew it. Nobody but the British can achieve quite that air of casual distinction. I am Mimi Paragon your cruise hostess.

SIR GERARD. Howdoyoudo?

MIMI. Howdoyoudo? It is my duty and pleasure to see that you enjoy every fascinating moment of this great, glamorous, gorgeous adventure. Do you care for Bingo?

SIR GERARD. Who is Bingo?

MIMI. Isn't that wonderful. And they say the British have no sense of humour. I do hope you will all do me the honour or coming to my little "Get Together" cocktail party at six o'clock tomorrow evening in the Winter Garden Lounge.

SIR GERARD. "Get Together" cocktail party?

MIMI. Don't say another word. The idea nauseates you, I can see it in your eye. I was a mad, crazy fool ever to think of it. I implore you to wipe the whole sordid suggestion from your mind. And Lady Nutfield, if there is one teeny, weeny thing I can do to make your voyage carefree, irresponsible and sheer heaven, just let me know. I can supply anything from a fourth at Bridge to an Alcohol rub. Arrivederci for the momento.

SIR GERARD. The woman's obviously a lunatic.

L. NUTFIELD. Oh dear. I was afraid this sort of thing might happen. Will you join us for a sherry, Mrs. Van Mier?

MIMI. *(going to* **BARNABY***)* I've never seen New Jersey looking lovelier, have you?

BARNABY. Actually, I've never seen New Jersey at all. I come from McKeesport, Pennsylvania.

MIMI. We must wipe the past from our minds and concentrate on the future. Are you travelling alone?

BARNABY. Yes.

MIMI. Thank God. I had a dreadful feeling that you might be one of a honeymoon couple. Honeymoon couples are disaster on a cruise. They only think of: one thing and it isn't shuffleboard. Are you the retiring type or are you willing to open wide your arms to adventure and savour life to the full?

BARNABY. I don't know, Ma'am. I've never thought about it.

MIMI. Don't be alarmed. I'm Mimi Paragon, your cruise hostess. Unattached young men are my natural prey. What's your name?

BARNABY. Barnaby…Barnaby Slade.

MIMI. Come on Barnaby…I'm gonna buy you a drink…I have a feeling you're going to need me.

[MUSIC #5: "COME TO ME – REPRISE"]

(singing)

AND IF YOU FEEL LONELY AND NEED A PAL
I'M THE GAL

TO TAKE YOU IN TOW

IF YOU'RE PINING FOR AFFECTION AND A SYMPATHETIC
FRIEND

I'VE A LARGE COLLECTION I CAN RECOMMEND

IF YOU WANT SOMETHING DISCREETLY PLANNED

ON THIS GRAND

AND GRACIOUS BATEAU

IF YOU'RE BASICALLY FRUSTRATED AND A MARTYR TO
ENNUI

COME TO ME – COME TO ME

OR IF YOU NEED A MARIJUANA OR A QUIET CUP OF TEA

COME TO ME LOST LAMB –

COME TO ME – LOST LAMB – COME TO ME!

(When **MIMI** *has gone off with* **BARNABY, JOHNNY**
*strolls down and stands at the lower rail left. He lights a
cigarette.* **MR. & MRS. SWEENEY** *come up to him.)*

MRS. SWEENEY. Aren't those little tugs the cutest things you
ever saw?

JOHNNY. *(vaguely)* Yes – yes they are.

*(**ALVIN** chases little girl P.S. – O.P.)*

MRS. SWEENEY. I am Mrs. Sweeney. This is my husband Mr.
Sweeney. This is the first time we've ever been on a
trip together and we've been married over fifty years –
haven't we, Edgar?

MR. SWEENEY. Yes sweetheart.

MRS. SWEENEY. *(presevering)* You'd never think that those
tiny little boats could turn a great big ship like this
right round, would you?

JOHNNY. *(without expression)* No. I don't suppose you would.

MRS. SWEENEY. *(giving up the struggle)* Well – bye-bye for now.

JOHNNY. *(forcing a smile)* Bye-bye.

MRS. SWEENEY. *(moving left)* Oh Mrs. Paragon.

MIMI. *(enter left)* Aren't those little tugs the sweetest thing
you ever saw?

*(**MIMI** comes up to **JOHNNY**.)*

I've never seen New Jersey looking lovelier, have you?

JOHNNY. I beg your pardon?

MIMI. Don't be alarmed. I'm Mimi Paragon, your cruise hostess.

JOHNNY. Oh, how do you do...

MIMI. It's part of my job to accost anyone who looks the teensiest weensiest bit lonely and make their life a living Hell. What's your name?

JOHNNY. Johnny – Johnny Van Mier.

MIMI. Of course, I should have guessed. You and your mother are down for VIP treatment...you know, Captain's table...a little extra fruit in the cabin, Do you care for deck tennis at all?

JOHNNY. Not very much.

MIMI. You're so right. However, I do hope you'll do me the honour of coming to my little "Get Together" cocktail party at six o'clock tomorrow evening in the Winter Garden Lounge?

JOHNNY. It's very nice of you to ask me. I'd love to.

MIMI. Sweet God I made it. I'll see you at six. Ciaou for now.

(blast from ship's whistle)

[MUSIC #6: "SAIL AWAY – REPRISE"]

JOHNNY. *(singing)*
WHEN YOU CAN'T HEAR THE CLAMOUR OF THE NOISY TOWN

ALL.
SAIL AWAY – SAIL AWAY!

JOHNNY.
WHEN THE FRIEND YOU HAD COUNTED ON HAS LET YOU DOWN

ALL.
SAIL AWAY – SAIL AWAY!

JOHNNY.
BUT WHEN SOON OR LATE

YOU RECOGNISE YOUR FATE
THAT WILL BE YOUR GREAT
GREAT DAY
ON THE WINGS OF THE MORNING WITH YOUR OWN TRUE
    LOVE
SAIL AWAY –

ALL.
SAIL AWAY –

JOHNNY.
LOOK AWAY!

Scene Three

(ELINOR SPENCER-BOLLARD's CABIN)

[MUSIC #6A: "SAIL AWAY – UTILITY"]

(When the lights fade in on the scene, **ELINOR SPENCER-BOLLARD** *is sitting on the bed reading aloud from a volume of poetry.* **NANCY FOYLE** *is on her knees on the floor unpacking a suitcase.)*

ELINOR. "When I have fears that I may cease to be
Before my pen has gleaned my teeming brain…"
The handkerchiefs can go with the stockings in the top drawer.

NANCY. Yes, Aunt Elinor.

ELINOR. "Before high piled books in character
Hold like rich garners the full-ripened grain."
That was Keats dear.

NANCY. Yes, Aunt Elinor.

ELINOR. You see, he was afraid he was going to die before he could write all there was in him to write. I sometimes feel like that myself, a sort of impotent rage against the impermanence of life. Where are my heart pills?

NANCY. I put them in the drawer by your bed.

ELINOR. It was kind of the Scarsdale Book of the Month Club to send me all those nuts. I don't know what we're going to do with them. Are you a good sailor?

NANCY. I don't know…I've never been on a ship before.

ELINOR. Well we must hope for the best. Sea-sickness is largely mental. Eating is also important. There's nothing like bulk to keep you steady. Are all my notes together?

NANCY. Yes. They're in here.

ELINOR. Dear Veronica always used coloured rubber bands, a different colour for each country. She was very methodical.

NANCY. Yes, Aunt Elinor, you told me. I've done the same.

ELINOR. Good girl. I'm sure we will get on famously. It's all a tremendous adventure, isn't it?

NANCY. Yes. I'm thrilled. I can hardly believe it.

ELINOR. Heigho! I'm going to take a little trot around the deck. Health comes first. "The world is too much with us, late and soon, getting and spending we lay waste our powers." I've never wasted a moment since the day I was born. What nonsense Wordsworth wrote sometimes, didn't he?

NANCY. I don't know. I've never read him.

ELINOR. Never read your Wordsworth? What a little ignoramus we are to be sure. *(kiss)* "The Rainbow comes and goes and lovely is the rose." Don't forget to tell the steward about my hot water bottle.

(**ELINOR** *exits.*)

[MUSIC #7: "WHERE SHALL I FIND HIM"]

NANCY. *(singing)*

OH, DARLING MOTHER THIS
WAS A MISTAKE. I CAN NEVER DO THE JOB.
I NEVER SHOULD HAVE COME
I'M FAR TOO DUMB.
I KNOW SHE'S GOING TO MISS
THAT OTHER GIRL, FOR AT LEAST SHE KNEW THE JOB.
CAN YOU IMAGINE HOW SHE'D RAGE AT ME
SHOULD SHE DISCOVER
I'M REALLY SEARCHING FOR A LOVER?

WHERE SHALL I FIND HIM?
WHERE WILL HE BE?
WHERE SHALL I FIND HIM
THE ONE FOR ME?

SUDDENLY, SUDDENLY, MAYBE WE'LL MEET
ON AN ORDINARY DAY, ON SOME ORDINARY
STREET
HOW SHALL I KNOW HIM?

WHAT WILL HE WEAR?
HOW SHALL I SHOW HIM
HOW TENDERLY I CARE?
HOW SHALL I PROVE TO HIM
MAKE HIM CLEARLY SEE
THAT HE'S THE ONLY ONE FOR ME.

[MUSIC #7A: "WHERE SHALL I FIND HER – UTILITY"]

Scene Four

(THE SUN DECK.)

(The ship has been at sea now for several days and the atmosphere on board is no longer strained with unfamiliarity and the excitement of leaving. Most of the **PASSENGERS** *know each other, at least by sight; cliques have been formed; incipient romances among the young have begun; people have adapted themselves gradually to a daily shipboard routine; the sea is calm and the sky is blue.)*

(The deck is dotted with **PASSENGERS** *in bikinis and bathing trunks chatting and sunning themselves.)*

(In deck chairs Stage Right are **MR. & MRS. SWEENEY***. Seated at the Bar Centre Stage are* **MRS. LUSH, ALVIN** *and* **MR. RAWLINGS***. The* **CANDIJACKS** *are taking snapshots at the bottom of the stairs to the Upper Deck.* **ELINOR SPENCER-BOLLARD** *is in a deck chair Stage Left.)*

SHIRLEY. All right now smile! There. I can't wind it, it's stuck!

ELINOR. *(calling)* Nancy. Nancy! Nancy! To work child, to work. Here's your pad, your pencil...ready?

*(***NANCY*** rushes on.)*

NANCY. Yes, Aunt Elinor.

ELINOR. Page 56, Chapter 5 Sylvia galloped into the paddock, her hair flying in the wind. Tracy helped her to dismount...

*(***MR. & MRS. SWEENEY*** come up to ***ELINOR***.)*

MRS. SWEENEY. Isn't a lovely morning?

ELINOR. Yes, yes it is.

MRS. SWEENEY. You'd never think we'd been at sea for five days would you?

ELINOR. No, no you wouldn't.

MRS. SWEENEY. Early this morning Mr. Sweeney looked out of the porthole and saw a whole school of porpoises. Didn't you Edgar?

MR. SWEENEY. Yes, sweetheart.

MRS. SWEENEY. At least the steward said they were porpoises…

(**SWEENEYS** *exit left.*)

ELINOR. That was a dull piece of information. "Tracy helped her to dismount, then, suddenly obeying an impulse too strong to be resisted, he crushed her to him. She gave a strangled cry and battered his sun-tanned chest impotently with her fists, but his arms were like steel bands around her quivering body." I'm a little uneasy about 'quivering body.'

NANCY. They have them in Trinidad, don't they?

ELINOR. What are you talking about?

NANCY. Steel bands. I've heard the records.

ELINOR. You must not interrupt, Nancy. It breaks the flow. "And the blood began pounding in her ears."

(**MRS. VAN MIER** *comes up to* **ELINOR.**)

MRS. MIER. Good morning.

ELINOR. Good morning.

MRS. MIER. Forgive me for disturbing you but I simply cannot resist the opportunity of telling you how much I've enjoyed all your delightful books.

ELINOR. Thank you, thank you, how very kind.

MRS. MIER. I am Mrs. Van Mier. My mother went to school with Edith Wharton, you know.

ELINOR. No, I didn't know.

MRS. MIER. They used to get up to all sorts of mischief together.

(*laughter from both*)

And my elder sister knew Pearl Buck intimately in Hong Kong, or was it Edna Ferber?

ELINOR. If it was Hong Kong it was Pearl Buck.

MRS. MIER. Perhaps you would join my son and me for luncheon one day?

ELINOR. I'm afraid I never eat luncheon. Just a baked potato and a glass of white wine.

MRS. MIER. How sensible, how sensible. Au revoir for the moment.

(**MRS. VAN MIER** *goes off.*)

ELINOR. Make a note, Nancy. "Mrs. Van Mier, celebrity snob, literary pretensions, hard as nails." Where were we?

NANCY. "And the blood began pounding in her ears."

(**MRS. LUSH** *and* **ALVIN** *walk by* **ELINOR.**)

ALVIN. Mom, why is that lady wearing that funny hat? She looks like a horse.

MRS. LUSH. Uhuh…yes!

(*Exit* **MRS. LUSH** *and* **ALVIN.**)

ELINOR. That child should be kept in a cage with its mother. Change quivering body to shrinking form. And her shoulder strap fell provocatively from her shoulder…

(**MIMI** *enters from right,* **RUNNER** *crosses from left.*)

MIMI. Ah, Mrs. Spencer-Ballard, working away as usual! You are indefatigable. I don't know how you do it.

ELINOR. I must admit I'm finding it increasingly difficult.

MIMI. I was wondering if I might persuade you to give a little talk one evening in the Winter Garden Lounge? I can assure you it would be deeply appreciated.

ELINOR. Really, Mrs. Paragon, I'm afraid…

MIMI. I implore you not to let that ghastly word 'No' fall from your lips, Mrs. Spencer-Bollard. We need you. I have had deputation after deputation begging me on their bended knees to ask you this great great favour.

ELINOR. My dear Mrs. Paragon I…

MIMI. Don't say anything now. Just consider it. Mull it over in your brilliant mind. Brood on it. You are a great woman, Mrs. Spencer-Ballard. You are loved and revered from the Rocky Mountains to the Mexican border. I suppose it's no use trying to interest you in the Shuffleboard Tournament?

ELINOR. It most certainly is not.

MIMI. You're so right. A woman or your intellectual calibre shoving away at those gruesome little disks. Quelle fantasie! Well, I must run now like a little hunted hare and tot up the bingo scores. Adiamo tutti.

(*as she exits:*)

Oh, boy…

ELINOR. Make a note Nancy. Professional hostess…too much vitality…wakes up cheerful…hates people, loves animals.

NANCY. Gee, I like her. It must be a terrible job having to cope with everybody and keep them amused.

ELINOR. Type out that chapter and come to me at two-thirty sharp. I'm going to the cabin…my inspiration has withered on the bough. I shall fold my tents like the Arabs and as silently steal away.

(**ELINOR** *stamps noisily off.*)

BARNABY. At last we are alone!

NANCY. Oh, it's you.

BARNABY. If I suddenly crushed you in my arms would you give a strangled cry?

NANCY. You've been listening.

BARNABY. Of course I have. I've been hiding behind a newspaper. Did you know that my great grandmother met Harriet Beecher Stowe at a Bar-B-Que?

NANCY. Don't be silly.

BARNABY. My Uncle Willy knows Tennessee Williams' psychiatrist intimately. They get up to all sorts of mischief together.

NANCY. I must go type these notes.

BARNABY. Does that old prune keep you at it all day long?

NANCY. She's not an old prune. She's a wonderful woman and one of the most distinguished writers in America.

BARNABY. You've got some freckles on your nose. I never noticed them before.

NANCY. Well it's very rude of you to notice them now.

BARNABY. But I love freckles...they send me. Hold still for just a minute. The light's perfect.

NANCY. Why do you keep on taking photographs of me? I'm not in the least bit celebrated or important.

BARNABY. How do you know? You might be the most important person in the world to someone some day.

NANCY. Well I'm not now.

BARNABY. Could I persuade you to give a brief informal talk on steel bands and sex in the engine room?

NANCY. No.

BARNABY. Steel bands send me almost as much as freckles do. They make me think of coral reefs, blue lagoons, bright colored birds and you lying in my arms staring up through coconut palms at the tropical stars.

NANCY. You've not only chosen the wrong girl, but the wrong cruise!

BARNABY. Everything's in the mind.

[MUSIC #8: "BEATNIK LOVE AFFAIR"]

(singing)

WHY SUFFER FROM MORAL CONVICTIONS?
SOCIAL RESTRICTIONS?
LET'S THUMB OUR NOSES AT
COLD WARS AND ATOMIC PREDICTIONS.
THEY'RE ONLY A WASTE OF TIME.
LET'S MAKE A ROMANTIC DECISION
FOLLOW A VISION
NOW IS THE MOMENT TO SEE CLEARLY
AND REALIZE THAT REALLY

WE ARE ON THE BRINK OF IT
COME TO THINK OF IT.

YOU AND I COULD HAVE AN UPRIGHT, DOWNRIGHT,
    WATERTIGHT, DYNAMITE
LOVE AFFAIR
WE COULD EITHER PLAY IT UP-BEAT, DOWNBEAT, ON-THE-
    BEAT, OFF-THE-BEAT,
FAIR OR SQUARE
HEY FOR THOSE FLIP CALYPSOS
HO FOR THAT RHYTHMIC DIN
HEIGHO FOR THOSE DOPES AND DIPSOS
RUM PUNCH, COCONUTS, GORDON'S GIN
THINK IF WE TRIED OUT
SOME LITTLE HIDE-OUT
ON SOME TROPICAL ISLE
NAKED AND WARM
FROM DAWN TO MOONRISE
SOMERSET MAUGHAM-WISE
BLUE LAGOON-WISE
WE COULD LIE UPON THE BEACH AT NIGHT DEAR
WATCHING ALL THOSE RUSSIAN SATELLITES DEAR

WHIZZING THROUGH THE AIR
WHILE WE CARRIED ON WITH OUR OFF-BEAT, ON-BEAT,
    BEATNIK
LOVE AFFAIR.
YOU AND I COULD HAVE AN IN-BOARD, OUTBOARD,
    OVERBOARD, BED-AND-BOARD
LOVE AFFAIR
ALL WE NEED'S A LITTLE OFF-KEY, ON-KEY, KING-SIZED,
    ORGANIZED
TIME TO SPARE
THERE BY THE CARIBBEAN
WE'LL CROSS THE RUBICON
WE'LL HAVE, BY THE DEEP BLUE SEA AN
ALL-OUT, ROUSTABOUT, CARRY-ON.

WE'LL GET A 'MAN-TAN'

GARGANTUAN TAN
ON THOSE SHIMMERING SANDS
NOTHING TO DO BUT READ AND REST DEAR
WE COULD GET THROUGH 'BY LOVE POSSESSED' DEAR
EVERYTIME WE HEAR A SEAGULL WHISTLE
WE'LL FORGET OUR LAST MISGUIDED MISSILE
JUST DESTROYED TIMES SQUARE
AS WE CARRY ON WITH OUR KING-SIZED, ORGANIZED,
BEATNIK LOVE AFFAIR

(dance)

BARNABY. *(spoken)* And so as the natives sink slowly into the sea, we bid farewell to our little island paradise. What d'ya say Nancy?

(dance)

*(End of dance. **CARRINGTON** enters striking a small chiming gong to announce lunch. **MRS. VAN MIER** enters from right and sits in deck chair. **MIMI** enters from left.)*

MIMI. Would it drive you completely insane if I sat down for a few minutes?

MRS. MIER. No, of course not.

MIMI. You always look so cool and unruffled. I feel as if I'd spent my entire life in a supermarket. I've just escorted a merry throng of rubbernecks around the ship, engine room and all. They do ask the damnedest questions.

MRS. MIER. Can you answer them?

MIMI. What I don't know I invent.

MRS. MIER. You certainly have chosen a most extraordinary profession. I can't say I envy you.

MIMI. Oh, it has its points. I see the world and get well paid for it.

MRS. MIER. Have you been doing it for long?

MIMI. Yes...ever since I retired from the stage...owing to popular demand.

MRS. MIER. Oh, I had no idea you were an actress.

MIMI. Neither had anyone else. That's why I ran away to sea. This is my seventh cruise in this gracious vessel. I'm beginning to feel as much a part of this ship as the funnel. What's that you're reading?

MRS. MIER. *Anna Karenina* it's one of my standbys.

MIMI. Now wait a minute. I saw a movie of that once. She throws herself under a train, doesn't she? All for l'amour?

MRS. MIER. Not entirely for l'amour as you call it, but because everything becomes too much for her.

MIMI. Well, let me know when the next train's passing. Everything is certainly becoming too much for me. There's been an angry scene about the deck tennis finals and our shuffleboard champion has developed a hernia.

(MRS. VAN MIER exits right. As ALVIN and MRS. LUSH enter from left, MIMI moves into MRS. VAN MIER's steamer chair and closes her eyes wearily.)

MRS. LUSH. It was all your own fault Alvin. If you hadn't thrown the little girl's doll down the ventilator she wouldn't have hit you with the bat, and if you don't behave yourself and learn to be a good boy mother will have you analyzed again.

(They exit right. JOHNNY enters from left.)

JOHNNY. Good morning.

MIMI. Buon Giorno.

JOHNNY. You're not feeling ill are you?

MIMI. No, why?

JOHNNY. It's the first time I've ever seen you sitting down.

MIMI. I've just been talking to your mother.

JOHNNY. Oh.

MIMI. I have a sneaking suspicion she doesn't quite approve of me.

JOHNNY. Don't worry. Mother always disapproves of anyone I happen to like.

MIMI. That should be a great comfort to you socially. Well, I have to go and check the ping pong finals.

JOHNNY. Don't go for a moment. I want to tell you something.

MIMI. What? What?

(She sits in the deck chair. **JOHNNY** *sits in a chair beside her.)*

JOHNNY. I want to tell you that I've never enjoyed anything in my life as much as dancing with you last night.

MIMI. That's very handsome of you, Mr. Van Mier. I enjoyed it too.

JOHNNY. You promised last night that you'd call me Johnny. All my friends call me Johnny.

MIMI. Okay, Johnny, but I really must go…

JOHNNY. Wait a minute. Did I talk an awful lot of nonsense last night?

MIMI. Of course not. We had a wonderful evening.

JOHNNY. It was the first time I felt really happy since I came on board.

MIMI. Well, maybe you're getting your sea legs.

JOHNNY. I'm not usually in the habit of pouring out my private troubles to people. I owe you a lot for being so understanding and wise.

MIMI. It's easy to be wise about other people.

JOHNNY. You suddenly look sad

MIMI. I must be slipping.

JOHNNY. Is your husband alive?

MIMI. That's a direct question and deserves an indirect answer. Yes and no.

JOHNNY. How do you mean?

MIMI. As far as he's concerned he's alive, as far as I'm concerned he isn't. We had a whirlwind divorce in 1957. Next question?

JOHNNY. I don't mean to be impertinent.

MIMI. Don't be silly… *(pause)* Tell me something Johnny, how old are you?

JOHNNY. Twenty-six, why?

MIMI. Nothing, I just wondered.

JOHNNY. Is age so important to you?

MIMI. It's beginning to be.

JOHNNY. I'm not a boy you know. I mean…I've been around quite a bit.

MIMI. So have I.

JOHNNY. Are you laughing at me?

MIMI. Maybe a little. You're an attractive guy Johnny, and you dance divinely…

JOHNNY. But what?

MIMI. But I don't think you should encourage yourself to think along the lines you are thinking at the moment.

JOHNNY. Why not?

[MUSIC #9: "LATER THAN SPRING"]

MIMI. Well, I am a little older than you are.

JOHNNY. Age again.

MIMI. Yes. It does keep popping up doesn't it.

JOHNNY. *(singing)*
HAVE NO FEARS FOR FUTURE YEARS
FOR SWEET COMPENSATION YOU MAY FIND
MAKE YOUR BOW
TO THE MOMENT THAT IS NOW
AND ALWAYS BEAR IN MIND.

LATER THAN SPRING
THE WARMTH OF SUMMER COMES
THE CHARM OF AUTUMN COMES
THE LEAVES ARE GOLD
POETS SAY
THAT THE BLOSSOMS OF MAY
FADE AWAY
AND DIE
YET, DON'T FORGET

THAT WE MET
WHEN THE SUN WAS HIGH.
LATER THAN SPRING
WORDS THAT WERE SAID BEFORE
TEARS THAT WERE SHED BEFORE
CAN BE CONSOLED
REALIZE THAT IT'S WISE TO REMEMBER
THOUGH TIME IS ON THE WING
SONG BIRDS STILL SING
LATER THAN SPRING.

LATER THAN SPRING
THOUGH CARELESS RAPTURE PAST
NO NEED TO GAZE AGHAST
AT DAYS GONE BY
IF YOU WILL YOU CAN STILL
FEEL THE THRILL
OF A NEW DESIRE
STILL REEL THAT GLOW
WHEN YOU KNOW THAT YOUR WORLD'S ON FIRE.

LATER THAN SPRING
REMEMBERED APRIL SHOWERS
MAY BRING OUR PRESENT HOURS
A CLEARER SKY
WE PRETEND AND PRETEND IT' S THE END
BUT THE PENDULUM MUST SWING
NIGHTINGALES SING
LATER THAN SPRING.

(They move left.)

(Enter **SIR GERARD NUTFIELD.***)*

SIR GERARD. Purser.

JOE. Good morning sir.

SIR GERARD. This is a British ship is it not?

JOE. Yes, sir.

SIR GERARD. Well, all I can say is, it doesn't feel like one.

JOE. I'm sorry to hear that sir.

SIR GERARD. In the first place it's crawling with Americans.

JOE. The whole cruise is organized for the American trade, sir.

SIR GERARD. And in the second place, I've just found a cockroach in my bath.

JOE. I trust it was a British cockroach, sir.

SIR GERARD. I am not accustomed to impertinence; on a British ship especially.

JOE. Correct, Sir. You are absolutely right, sir.

SIR GERARD. Thank you purser. Come Mildred, time for luncheon,

[MUSIC #10: "THE PASSENGER'S ALWAYS RIGHT"]

(**NUTFIELDS** *exit left. The* **STEWARDS** *enter one by one.*)

CARRINGTON. *(singing)*
THE WOMAN IN CABIN FORTY-NINE HAS LOST HER
    DIAMOND BROOCH.

JOE.
CALM HER CARRINGTON
CHARM HER CARRINGTON
THAT'S THE CORRECT APPROACH.

HOSKINS.
A GENTLEMAN ON THE PROMENADE DECK JUST CALLED ME
    A LAZY SLOB.

JOE.
SMILE AT HIM HOSKINS
SMILE AT HIM HOSKINS
THAT IS PART OF YOUR JOB.

STEWARD.
THE THREE FAT CHILDREN IN B DECK, 3
HAVE THROWN THEIR BATH-MAT IN THE SEA.

S'WORTH.
THE SILLY OLD BROAD IN MAIN DECK TWO
HAS DROPPED HER DENTURES DOWN THE LOO.

JOE.

> PASSENGERS SINCE THE WORLD BEGAN
> HAVE BEEN QUERULOUS, RUDE AND SNOOTY
> ENGLAND EXPECTS THAT EVERY MAN
> THIS DAY, SHOULD DO HIS DUTY.
> Weatherby?

WEATHERBY. Here.

JOE. Hoskins?

HOSKINS. Here.

JOE. Green, Blake, Richardson?

GREEN, BLAKE & RICHARDSON. Here. Here. Here.

JOE. Crawford?

CRAWFORD. Here.

JOE. Shuttleworth?

SHUTTLEWORTH. Here.

JOE. Smith, Brown, Parkinson?

SMITH, BROWN & PARKINSON. Here. Here. Here.

JOE. Where the devil are Bruce and Frome?

HOSKINS. One's got shingles and the other's gone home.

JOE. Where's O'Reilley and Jock McBride?

GREEN, BLAKE & RICHARDSON. One got married, the other got fried.

JOE. Carrington?

CARRINGTON. Here.

JOE. Brewster?

BREWSTER. Here.

JOE. Where's young Fawcett and Windermere?

WEATHERBY. Fawcett stayed home in bed.

STEWARDS. Poor old Windermere dropped down dead.

JOE.

> IN THE COURSE OF EACH CRUISE
> I ALWAYS CHOOSE
> TO LECTURE EACH SUBORDINATE
> YOU'RE NOT DAMNED FOOLS
> AND YOU KNOW THE RULES

SO SEE YOU ALL CO-ORDINATE.

STEWARDS.

WE'VE HEARD ALL THIS BEFORE.

HOSKINS.

I CAN'T STAND ANY MORE.

JOE.

BOW, SMILE, CHARM, TACT.
NEVER FORGET ONE VITAL FACT.

THE PASSENGER'S ALWAYS RIGHT MY BOYS
THE PASSENGER'S ALWAYS RIGHT
ALTHOUGH HE'S A DRIP
HE'S PAID FOR HIS TRIP
SO GREET HIM WITH DELIGHT
AGREE TO ALL SUGGESTIONS
HOWEVER COARSE OR CRUDE
REPLY TO ALL HIS QUESTIONS
PLY HIM WITH DRINK – STUFF HIM WITH FOOD
THE PASSENGER MAY BE SOBER BOYS
THE PASSENGER MAY BE TIGHT
THE PASSENGER MAY BE FOE OR FRIEND
OR ABSOLUTELY ROUND THE BEND
BUT CALM HIM
CHARM HIM
EVEN THOUGH HE'S HIGHER THAN A KITE
THE PASSENGER'S ALWAYS RIGHT.

THE PASSENGER'S ALWAYS RIGHT MY BOYS
THE PASSENGER'S ALWAYS RIGHT
THOSE DREARY OLD WRECKS
WHO LITTER THE DECKS
DEMAND THAT YOU'RE POLITE
DON'T COUNT ON ANY FREE TIME
BE KIND TO ALL THE JERKS
AND EVERY DAY AT TEA TIME
STUFF 'EM WITH CAKE...GIVE 'EM THE WORKS
THE PASSENGER MAY BE DULL BOYS
THE PASSENGER MAY BE BRIGHT

THE PASSENGER MAY BE QUITE SERENE
OR GIBBERING WITH BENZEDRINE
BUT NURSE HIM
CURSE HIM
ONLY WHEN THE BASTARD'S OUT OF SIGHT
REMEMBER BOYS
THE GODDAMNED PASSENGER'S ALWAYS

HOSKINS.

RIGHT. RIGHT.

GREEN.

RIGHT. RIGHT.

CARRINGTON.

RIGHT. RIGHT.

BLAKE.

RIGHT. RIGHT.

HOSKINS, GREEN, CARRINGTON & BLAKE.

WE'RE PASSENGERS, AND WE'RE RIGHT MY BOYS,
WE'RE PASSENGERS AND WE'RE RIGHT!

JOE.

THEY' RE RIGHT!

HOSKINS, GREEN, CARRINGTON & BLAKE.

WE'RE RIGHT, WE'RE RIGHT, WE'RE RIGHT!

HOSKINS.

I'M RIGHT, I'M RIGHT, I'M RIGHT!

JOE.

REMEMBER BOYS, THE GODDAMNED PASSENGER'S ALWAYS
RIGHT!

[MUSIC #10A: "PASSENGER'S – UTILITY"]

Scene Five

(MIMI'S CABIN)

*(**MIMI** in dressing gown and slippers, is seated in a chair with an Italian Lesson book on her knees. She occasionally glances at herself in the mirror which is on the table by her side.)*

MIMI. *(ad lib)* Ascolte mi – apporte mi un martini molta molta secco subito – me piacere. Thanks Fred. *(to her own reflection)* Io sono molta bella – *(She glances at the book.)* Io non sono molta bella – *(She looks back at the mirror.)* I was right the second time. *(She turns to* **ADLAI** *in his basket.)* Adlai Lei e uno molto bello poodlino, that's what lei e.

(There is a knock at the door.)

Come in.

*(**JOE** comes in. He is carrying a corsage or flowers.)*

JOE. I've brought you some flowers, to boost your morale at the prize-giving tonight.

MIMI. Why, Joe – that's just the sweetest thing I've ever known. *(She jumps up, takes the flowers and embraces him.)* You're an angel.

JOE. They'll bring out the colour in your eyes.

MIMI. Much better leave it where it is.

JOE. Come and have a snifter in my cabin before dinner. Shuttleworth's wife's just had another baby – we're celebrating.

MIMI. Poor Shuttleworth – I can't think where he gets the time.

JOE. See you in about half an hour?

MIMI. Okay. Thanks for the flowers. You're a real pal. *(**JOE** goes out).*

(phone rings)

MIMI. *(cont.)* Pronto. Pronto. Ah, Mrs. Sweeney, yes, Mrs. Sweeney, no, Mrs. Sweeney...by all means, Mrs. Sweeney. Yes, the shuffleboard winners will be announced after dinner and the prizes will be awarded in the main lounge at ten-thirty. No Mrs. Sweeney, Capt. Wilberforce' s Gala Dinner is day after tomorrow. Just ordinary evening dress for tonight. No, Mrs. Sweeney no paper hats. Yes, Mrs. Sweeney if the steward said they were porpoises, they sure were porpoises, all our stewards are trained to recognize porpoises instantaneously. Arriverderci Mrs. Sweeney. *(she reads from book)* "How much are these boot-trees? Quanta costa quests..." Boot-trees? To hell with that. "I want five tickets for 'La Sonambula.'" Voglio cinque bigliette...

(phone rings)

Pronto. Ah, Mrs. Lush, I'm sure I'm very sorry, Mrs. Lush but it really was dear little Alvin's own fault you know. He was getting in everyone's way and they were playing the finals. Where did the rubber ring hit him? Oh, I see...poor little chap...Well, we must all hope it goes down by the morning I'm sure Mr. Fluger didn't do it on purpose, he's a family man and devoted to children. No, Mrs. Lush, they can't play deck tennis with sort rubber rings, they have to be hard. Very well, Mrs. Lush.

(She hangs up.)

(Jiggles receiver) Sylvia, be an angel and don't put any more calls through until I've learnt Italian. Si, si... Avanti Garibaldi! *(Reading from book)* "There is nothing to touch the English Strawberry." "I fear that this washing machine is of an inferior quality." Useful Phrases hey?

(She throws book.)

[MUSIC #11: "USEFUL PHRASES"]

MIMI. *(singing)*

WHEN THE TOWER OF BABEL FELL
IT CAUSED A LOT OR UNNECESSARY HELL
PERSONAL 'RAPPORT'
BECAME A COMPLICATED BORE
AND A LOT MORE DIFFICULT THAN IT HAD BEEN BEFORE
WHEN THE TOWER OF BABEL FELL.

THE CHINKS AND THE JAPS
AND THE FINNS AND LAPPS
WERE REDUCED TO A HALPLESS STAMMER
AND THE ANCIENT GREEKS TOOK AT LEAST SIX WEEKS
TO LEARN THEIR LATIN GRAMMAR
THE GUTTURAL WHEEZE
OF THE PORTUGUESE
FILLED THE BRAINS OF THE DANES
WITH HORROR
AND VERBS, NOT LUST
CAUSED THE FINAL BUST
IN SODOM AND GOMORRAH.

IF IT HADN'T BEEN FOR THAT
BLOODY BUILDING FALLING FLAT
I WOULD NOT HAVE HAD TO LEARN ITALIANO
AND KEEP MUTTERING 'SI, SI'
AND 'MI CHIAMANO MIMI'
LIKE AN AGING METROPOLITAN SOPRANO!

I SHOULD NOT HAVE HAD TO LOOK
AT THAT GHASTLY LITTLE BOOK
'TIL MY BRAIN BECOMES AS SOFT AS MAYONNAISE IS
MESSRS. HUGO AND BERLITZ
MUST HAVE TORN THEMSELVES TO BITS
DREAMING UP SO MANY USELESS, USEFUL PHRASES,

PRAY TELL ME THE TIME
IT IS SIX
IT IS SEVEN

IT'S HALF PAST ELEVEN
IT'S TWENTY TO TWO
I WANT THIRTEEN STAMPS
DOES YOUR CHILD HAVE CONVULSIONS
PLEASE BRING ME SOME RHUBARB
I NEED A SHAMPOO
HOW MUCH IS THAT HAT?

I DESIRE SOME RED STOCKINGS
MY MOTHER IS MARRIED
THESE BOOTS ARE TOO SMALL
MY AUNT HAS A COLD
SHALL WE GO TO THE OPERA
THIS MEAT IS DISGUSTING
IS THIS THE TOWN HALL?

MY COUSIN IS DEAR
KINDLY BRING ME A HATCHET
PRAY PASS ME THE PEPPER
WHAT PRETTY CRETONNE
WHAT TIME IS THE TRAIN
IT IS LATE
IT IS EARLY
IT'S RUNNING ON SCHEDULE
IT'S HERE
IT HAS GONE
I'VE WRITTEN SIX LETTERS
I'VE WRITTEN NO LETTERS
PRAY FETCH ME A HORSE
I HAVE NEED OF A GROOM
THIS ISN'T MY PASSPORT
THIS ISN'T MY HATBOX
PLEASE SHOW ME THE WAY
TO NAPOLEON'S TOMB.

THE WEATHER IS COOLER
THE WEATHER IS HOTTER
PRAY FASTEN MY CORSETS

PLEASE BRING ME MY CLOAK
I'VE LOST MY UMBRELLA
I'M IN A GREAT HURRY
I'M GOING
I'M STAYING
D'YOU MIND IF I SMOKE?
THIS MUTTON IS TOUGH
THERE'S A MOUSE IN MY BEDROOM
THIS EGG IS DELICIOUS

THIS SOUP IS TOO THICK
PLEASE BRING ME A TROUT
WHAT AN EXCELLENT PUDDING
PRAY HAND ME MY GLOVES
I'M GOING TO BE SICK!

[MUSIC #11A: "COME TO ME – UTILITY"]

Scene Six

BARNABY. Why are you suddenly mad at me?

NANCY. I just don't happen to like being pawed about.

BARNABY. If you didn't expect to be kissed why did you come up onto the boat deck in the moonlight?

NANCY. I did not expect to be kissed. I expected you to behave yourself...

BARNABY. How can you hope to wander about at night in a dress like that and not bring out the beast in men?

NANCY. You're not a man. You're nothing but an overgrown schoolboy, and fresh at that.

BARNABY. Will you have a Coca-cola with me in the bar before lunch tomorrow?

NANCY. No.

BARNABY. Will you come to the movies with me tomorrow afternoon at four-thirty? It's Joshua Logan's "Fanny" on a wide screen?

NANCY. No.

BARNABY. I knew it!

NANCY. Knew what?

BARNABY. You're crazy about me. But your sub-conscious won't let you admit it. You're scared.

NANCY. I'm not in the least scared.

BARNABY. Oh yes you are. You're scared that the naked, burning passion in my eyes might shrivel you up into a little freckled cinder

NANCY. Drop dead!

(She exits right.)

BARNABY. She loves me!

[MUSIC #12: "WHERE SHALL I FIND HER – REPRISE"]

(singing)

MAYBE I'VE FOUND HER
CAN THIS BE SHE?

MAYBE I'VE FOUND HER
THE ONE FOR ME
SUDDENLY, SUDDENLY I WONDER WHY
SUCH A LOT OF EXTRA STARS
SEEM TO SHIMMER IN THE SKY
CAN THIS BE MY GIRL
DO YOU SUPPOSE
THIS RATHER SHY GIRL
WITH FRECKLES ON HER NOSE
HOW CAN I PROVE TO HER
MAKE HER CLEARLY SEE
THAT SHE'S THE ONLY LOVE FOR ME?

(dance)

*[MUSIC #12A: "WHERE SHALL I FIND HER –
UTILITY"]*

Scene Seven

(THE SHIP'S NURSERY)

(The nursery is cheerfully designed for the very young. On Stage Right there is a slide and on Stage Left a merry-go-round.)

(As the lights fade in on the scene, the **CHILDREN** *are running in all directions and shrieking. The noise is deafening.)*

[MUSIC #13: "A.B.C. INTRO"]

*(***MIMI** *is sitting smoking a cigarette and making notes as she sits on a piano bench Stage Center. Next to her is a large air-filled animal to which* **ALVIN** *has tied a* **LITTLE GIRL***. He runs to* **MIMI** *and borrows her cigarette lighter and starts to set light to the* **LITTLE GIRL***.* **MIMI** *looks up, notices what he is doing, and stops him just in time.)*

(The noise continues until **MIMI***, after several unsuccessful attempts, manages to control the clamoring* **THRONG***.*

MIMI. That's quite enough of that. Be quiet all of you. I said QUIET. My darlings.

CASSIDY. Your heir's all mussed up.

MIMI. Yes dear I know it is. Now if you'll all gather round me and keep still I'll tell you a story.

ALVIN. Not the one about the honeymoon couple?

MIMI. No Alvin. Not the one about the honeymoon couple.

*(***CHILDREN** *run around screaming wildly.* **MIMI** *slams piano bench which stops them.)*

CASSIDY. I don't want to hear a story. I want to play I'm in a space ship.

MIMI. I wish to God you were…dear. *(He sneezes.)* God bless you.

ALVIN. Woolawoola woolawoolawoola I'm going to scalp Cynthia.

MIMI. Alvin…you can scalp Cynthia later. Just be a good boy and sit down and listen.

"Once upon a time

In a big dark wood

Lived a dear little girl

Who was very very good…"

ALVIN. Aw nuts!

MIMI. What did you say Alvin?

ALVIN. I said 'Nuts!'

MIMI. Well try not to sey it again

"One day a Prince came riding by

And what do you think he did?"

ALVIN. Spat in her eye!

(**CHILDREN** *once again break into screaming laughter and are stopped by* **MIMI** *slamming the piano bench.*)

[MUSIC #14: "A.B.C.'S"]

MIMI. *(singing)*

A.B.C,D.E.F.G.

H.I.J,K,L.M.N.O.

OH WHAT A JOLLY LITTLE JOCULAR

GROUP WE ARE

ALVIN. Bla, bla, bla!

MIMI.

VOCALIZE AND HARMONIZE

WHEN MOTHER CRIES

ONE, TWO, THREE GO

TRY, IF IT'S POSSIBLE TO KEEP ON KEY

SING THE LETTERS AFTER ME.

ALVIN. Just how corny can you be?

MIMI.

IF YOU SING WHEN YOU ARE BLUE

YOU FIND YOU

NEVER HAVE TO CARE A RAP

WHEN THE SKIES ARE DARK AND GREY

YOU JUST SAY

ALVIN. What a lot of –

MIMI. Alvin!

P.Q.R.S.T.U.V.

AND W.X.Y.Z. OR ZEE

THIS IS MY PERSONAL RECIPE

FOR THE LITTLE ONES' A.B.C.

A. STANDS FOR ABSOLUTELY ANYTHING

B. STANDS FOR BIG BRASS BANDS

C. STANDS FOR CHLOROPHYLL

D. STANDS FOR DEXAMIL

E. STANDS FOR ENDOCRINE GLANDS

F. AND G. DON'T SUGGEST A THING TO ME

NOR DO H.I.J.K.L.

BUT AFTER L. COMES M. FOR MOTHER

(**ALVIN** *gives a very large raspberry.*)

AND MOTHER'S GOING TO GIVE YOU HELL.

ALVIN.

A.

MIMI.

STANDS FOR ARTICHOKES AND ADENOIDS

BRIDGETT.

B.

MIMI.

STANDS FOR BOLTS AND BELTS.

CHRIS.

C.

MIMI.

STANDS FOR COTTAGE CHEESE.

DENNIS.

D.

MIMI.

STANDS FOR DUNGAREES.

ALVIN.

E.

MIMI.

STANDS FOR ANYTHING ELSE

MARY ELLEN.

G.

MIMI.

OF COURSE STANDS FOR GETTING A DIVORCE.

CASSIDY.

AND F.

MIMI.

SOMETIMES STANDS FOR FRIDGE.

CHILDREN. *(running to her)*

FRIDGE?

MIMI.

BUT IF I REALLY WERE YOUR MOTHER

I'D THROW MYSELF FROM BROOKLYN BRIDGE.

CHILDREN. *(marching around her)*

A. STANDS FOR ABSOLUTELY ANYTHING

B. STANDS FOR BIG BRASS BANDS

C. STANDS FOR CHLOROPHIL

D. STANDS FOR DEXAMIL

E. STANDS FOR ENDOCRINE GLANDS

F. AND G. DON'T SUGGEST A THING TO ME.

*(**CHILDREN** with H, O, R, E, cards line up. **ALVIN** has the W, and **DENNIS** the S.)*

NOR DO H.I.J.K.L.

BUT AFTER L. COMES M. FOR MOTHER

MIMI. *(As **ALVIN** starts to the head of the line)* Alvin…keep walking Alvin…Dennis, come in here with that S. Oh, boy!

BRIDGETT.

A.

MIMI.

STANDS FOR ROMEO AND JULIET

KIDS.

B.

MIMI.

STANDS FOR KU KLUX KLAN

KIDS.

C.

MIMI.

STANDS FOR BETHLEHEM.

KIDS.

D.

MIMI.

STANDS FOR M.G.M.

ALVIN.

E.

MIMI.

STANDS FOR 'SO'S YOUR OLD MAN.'

KIDS.

F. AND G. STAND FOR HOME IN TENNESSEE
AND WE KNOW H. STANDS FOR STOATS.

BRIDGETT.

BUT AFTER L. COMES M. FOR MIMI.

(**BRIDGETT** *takes* **MIMI** *downstage to show her cards.
As* **MIMI** *hugs* **BRIDGETT**, **ALVIN** *changes "Mimi" to
"Wiwi"…* **MIMI** *chases him around and down the slide.*)

Scene Eight

(THE PROMENADE DECK)

(The deck is empty. It is very late. **MIMI** *enters Downstage Right with six dogs.)*

MIMI. *(enters from right with dogs)* All right all of you, there's no use dragging back. You've been three times round the ship and it's time for you to go back to your baskets and dream those ghastly little dreams that make you twitch. And if any of you are planning in your evil little minds to make the smallest little wee-wee on this spotless deck, mother will wallop the living daylights out of you. Adlai stop looking at Skidder like that, you'll give her the wrong impression. Come on now, we're all going to our rooms.

*(***JOHNNY*** *enters from right.)*

JOHNNY. Mimi. I've been looking all over for you.

MIMI. You should have tried the kennels.

JOHNNY. Is this part of your job, too?

MIMI. A woman's work is never done.

*(***CARRINGTON*** *enters.)*

Oh, Carrington, be a darling and take our four-footed friends back to the Sun Deck. They've done everything they should and success is going to their heads.

CARRINGTON. Okay, Mimi.

MIMI. Oh, Carrington, are all the children tucked in bed?

CARRINGTON. Yes, I think so.

MIMI. None of them has fallen overboard?

CARRINGTON. Not yet.

MIMI. Well, we mustn't lost hope.

*(***CARRINGTON*** *exits right with dogs.)*

Could you let me have a cigarette?

JOHNNY. I waited for you in the bar until they threw me out.

MIMI. I'm sorry, Johnny, I just couldn't make it.

JOHNNY. I think we're getting near land, I can sort of feel it...a change in the air.

MIMI. Yes, I can feel it too.

JOHNNY. A lot seems to have changed for me in the last twenty-four hours.

MIMI. I really must go to bed...I'm worn out.

JOHNNY. Look there's a shooting star...we should make a wish.

MIMI. There's no time...it's gone.

JOHNNY. I had time. But the wish was already there. It's been there all evening.

MIMI. Good night Johnny.

JOHNNY. Don't go for a minute. I've got something very important to tell you.

MIMI. It can wait until the morning, can't it?

JOHNNY. No it can't. You know damn well it can't.

MIMI. Extinguish your cigarettes, fasten your seat belts, we are about to land.

JOHNNY. Why do you always make jokes.

MIMI. I'm paid to make jokes. I also have a very strong sense of self-preservation. Please don't be angry with me Johnny. I'm flattered and touched by what you want to say to...any woman would be...but I'd so much rather you didn't say it.

JOHNNY. Why?

MIMI. I don't know, there are a lot of reasons.

JOHNNY. Mimi, I know you've probably been unhappy and disappointed and disillusioned in your life but surely not enough to keep you from ever loving anyone again...even for a little.

MIMI. 'Even for a little'? A curiously practical phrase. Good-night Johnny.

(She exits right.)

[MUSIC #13: "GO SLOW JOHNNY"]

JOHNNY. *(singing)*

GO SLOW JOHNNY
MAYBE SHE'LL COME TO HER SENSES
IF YOU GIVE HER A CHANCE
PEOPLE'S FEELINGS ARE SENSITIVE PLANTS
TRY NOT TO TRAMPLE THE SOIL AND SPOIL ROMANCE.

GO SLOW JOHNNY
NO SENSE IN RUSHING YOUR FENCES
'TIL YOU KNOW THAT YOU KNOW
YOUR STARS ARE BRIGHT FOR YOU
RIGHT FOR YOU
MARK THEIR COURSES
HOLD YOUR HORSES
SPEAK LOW JOHNNY
TIP TOE JOHNNY
GO SLOW JOHNNY
GO SLOW.

GO SLOW JOHNNY
SLOW GOES IT
WAIT A BIT JOHNNY
THERE'S NO NEED TO STAMPEDE
DON' T FORGET IF YOU WISH TO SUCCEED
ONE TRUTH HAD BETTER BE FACED
MORE HASTE, LESS SPEED
WATCH THOSE ROAD SIGNS

THEY'LL INDICATE A BIT JOHNNY
WHICH DIRECTION TO GO
RELY ON TIME AND TACT
FACE THE FACT
YOU'RE NO BRANDO
RALLENTANDO

SPEAK LOW JOHNNY

TIP TOE JOHNNY
GO SLOW JOHNNY
GO SLOW
GO SLOW JOHNNY
GO SLOW!

(exit)

[MUSIC #14A: "GO SLOW SOCIETY"]

Scene Nine

(THE SUN DECK [NIGHT])

(The Sun Deck is gaily illuminated with coloured lights. The ship's orchestra is playing on the Upper Deck while the Lower Deck is crowded with **DANCING COUPLES** *in evening clothes and paper hats. Among them are* **MRS. LUSH** *and* **MR. RAWLINGS, MR. & MRS. SWEENEY, MR. & MRS. CANDIJACK, SIR GERARD** *and* **LADY NUTFIELD**, *and* **NANCY** *and* **GLEN.**)*

*(***CANDIJACK, ELINOR SPENCER-BOLLARD** *is seated Upstage Right staring vacantly into space and holding a drink in her hand.* **BARNABY** *cuts In on* **NANCY** *and* **GLEN.**)*

NANCY. Barnaby, if you don't stop cutting in every time I dance with somebody, I'm going to scream!

BARNABY. You said this afternoon at the movies that you'd dance with me and nobody else.

NANCY. Well I've changed my mind. It's a woman's what-d'you-call-it to change her mind.

BARNABY. Prerogative.

NANCY. My, my, my you do know a lot of long words don't you. You ought to dance with Aunt Elinor; she'd really appreciate you.

BARNABY. You're nothing but a heartless coquette.

NANCY. What' s that?

BARNABY. It's French.

NANCY. I don't care if it's Chinese…what does it mean?

BARNABY. It means a callous girl who plays fast and loose with the hearts of men and leads them into ruin and depravity and degradation.

NANCY. If that's the sort of girl you think I am I don't see why you want to dance with me at all.

BARNABY. I never will again. You're destroying me.

(He exits left.)

[MUSIC #15: "ACT ONE – FINALE"]

NANCY. Barnaby…Barnaby!

(She follows after him.)

MRS. MIER. *(to* ELINOR*)* Have you seen my son anywhere? I've been searching for him all over the ship.

ELINOR. "Thou art gone from my gaze like a beautiful dream

'And I seek thee in vain by the meadow and stream"

MRS. MIER. That is hardly a concise answer to my question.

*(*JOHNNY *comes on from the left with* MIMI. *They are both laughing.)*

MRS. MIER. Oh there you are Johnny. I've been looking for you everywhere.

JOHNNY. We've been having a drink in the smoking room.

MRS. MIER. I'm just on my way to bed. I only wanted to say good-night.

JOHNNY. Good-night mother.

MRS. MIER. *(kissing him)* Good-night dear. Don't stay up until all hours.

(She turns to MIMI *with a slight hardening of expression.)*

Good-night, Mrs. Paragon.

MIMI. Good-night, Mrs. Van Mier.

MRS. MIER. I admire your energy, I really do. I can't imagine how you keep it up.

(She gives a catty little laugh and goes off.)

MIMI. *(looking after her, a trifle ruefully)* I have a feeling your mother is just crazy about me.

JOHNNY. Now then – none of that.

(The music strikes up again.)

Come and dance.

(They start to dance. JOE *comes on hurriedly and goes up to* MIMI. *She stops dancing and steps downstage with*

him. He speaks to her for a moment. She laughs and beckons to **JOHNNY**.)

MIMI. This is it – This is it.

JOHNNY. What?

MIMI. *(She runs over to the band.)* Stop the music – Stop the music – Stop the music. *(The music stops with a jangle of chords.)* Land at last. Land at last. Look everybody, Europe! *(fanfare)* A bright light shining in a bad old world.

FANFARE.

(singing)

HAIL PIONEERS! HAIL PIONEERS! HAIL PIONEERS!
YOU HAVE SURVIVED.

ALL.

WE HAVE ARRIVED! WE HAVE ARRIVED! WE HAVE ARRIVED!

MIMI.

GIVE THANKS TO HIM, THIS BLESSED DAY
TO ONE ABOVE, WHO SET THE COURSE
I AM REFERRING NEED I SAY
TO CAPTAIN WILBERFORCE.

ALL.

ALL PRAISE TO HIM
ALL PRAISE TO HIM
WE HEARTILY ENDORSE
YOUR MOST APPROPRIATE SALUTE
TO CAPTAIN WILBERFORCE
YOUR MOST APPROPRIATE SALUTE
TO CAPTAIN WILBERFORCE.

MIMI.

YOU ARE ABOUT TO LAND
TOMORROW MORNING
UPON AN ALIEN STRAND
YOUR FEET WILL TREAD
ACCEPT FROM ME I PRAY
A FINAL WARNING
REMEMBER WHAT I SAY

REMEMBER WHAT I SAY
REMEMBER WHAT I'VE SAID…

YOU'RE A LONG LONG WAY FROM AMERICA
YOU'RE A LONG LONG WAY FROM HOME
LET THE STANDARD GUIDE BOOKS
BE YOUR BEDSIDE BOOKS
AND DON'T READ SNIDE BOOKS
LIKE 'THE LAYS OF ANCIENT ROME'
IF YOU'RE NOT PUT OFF
BY THE CONTINENTAL COFFEE
THAT ARRIVES ON YOUR BREAKFAST TRAY
YOU WILL FIND YOU'VE LEARNED A LITTLE FROM THE BAD
    OLD WORLD
WHEN YOU'RE BACK IN THE U.S.A

MIMI, NANCY & BARNABY.

YOU'RE A LONG, LONG WAY FROM AMERICA
BE PREPARED TO FACE THE WORST

MIMI.

WHILE GUITARS ARE STRUMMING
THE YANKS ARE COMING
YOU'LL FIND THE PLUMBING
RATHER FRIGHTENING AT FIRST
YOU NEED NOT SUSPECT
IF YOU'VE HAD ENOUGH INJECTIONS
EVERY FISH DISH THAT COMES YOUR WAY.

ALL.

YOU'LL HAVE LEARNED A LITTLE SOMETHING FROM THE
    BAD OLD WORLD
WHEN YOU'RE BACK IN THE U.S.A.

MIMI. *(spoken)*

GET OUT THE GREENBACKS!

ALL. *(spoken)*

GET OUT THE GREENBACKS!

ALL. *(singing)*

GET OUT THE GREENBACKS
GET OUT THE GREENBACKS
THEY WILL EXTRICATE US

IF WE SHOULD GO ASTRAY

MIMI. *(spoken)*

TOURISTS TOGETHER!

ALL.

IN ANCIENT NATIONS
THE POPULATIONS
HAVE LEARNED TO COUNT UPON
AMERICAN DONATIONS.

MIMI.

TRAVELER'S CHECKS CAN
DO MORE THAN SEX CAN
TO CONSOLIDATE US

ALL.

DON'T LET THE STATUS QUO GO
HAND OUT THOSE DOLLAR BILLS
BE LOYAL, BRAVE AND TRUE
TO THE TRADITIONS OF THE U.S.A.

MIMI.

ALL TOGETHER NOW!

ALL.

THEY WILL EXTRICATE US
IF WE SHOULD GO ASTRAY
IN ANCIENT NATIONS
THE POPULATIONS
HAVE LEARNED TO COUNT UPON
AMERICAN DONATIONS
TRAVELERS CHECKS CAN
DO MORE THAN SEX CAN
TO CONSOLIDATE US
DON'T LET THE STATUS QUO GO
HAND OUT THOSE DOLLAR BILLS

BE LOYAL, BRAVE AND TRUE
TO THE TRADITIONS OF THE U.S.A.

YOU'RE A LONG LONG WAY FROM AMERICA
BE PREPARED FOR STRESS AND STRAIN

DON'T EXPECT HOT SHOWERS
OR SEARCH FOR HOURS
TO FIND FRESH FLOWERS
THAT ARE WRAPPED IN CELLOPHANE
YOU NEED NOT SUSPECT
IF YOU'VE HAD ENOUGH INJECTIONS
EVERY FISH DISH THAT COMES YOUR WAY

YOU'LL HAVE LEARNED SOME HINTS ON COOKING IN THE
    BAD OLD WORLD
WHEN YOU'RE BACK IN THE U.
WHEN YOU'RE BACK IN THE U.
WHEN YOU'RE BACK IN THE U.S.
BACK IN THE U.S.A.
BACK IN THE U.S.A.

(**MIMI** *holds up flag.*)

End of Act One

ACT TWO

[MUSIC #16: "ENTR'ACTE"]

(TANGIERS)

(The scene is a 'Place' in Tangiers. On the left of the stage is a cafe with a table or two set under a coloured awning. Upstage Centre and stage Right are counters filled with Moroccan souvenirs and dry goods, At the back of the stage can be seen the Moorish buildings of the Kasbah.)

(At the end of the Second Act Overture a kind of Arab wailing begins and when the curtain rises there are several Arabian **VENDORS** *in long robes and turbans darting quickly about the stage.* **ALI**, *a disreputable-looking Arab, appears.)*

ALI. Ibrahim?

IBRAHIM. Here.

ALI. Stefanos?

STEFANOS. Here.

ALI. Scarface Molyneux?

SCARFACE. Here Boss. Here.

ALI. Heinrich?

HEINRICH. Ya.

ALI. Stanislas?

STANISLAS. Da.

ALI. Levi Finkelstein?

LEVI. Rah rah rah!

ALI. Where is Pedro the Portuguese?

STEFANOS & STANISLAS. In Gibraltar with a touch of D.T.S.

ALI. Where the devil is Wang-Hi Chung?

LEVI, IBRAHIM, HEINRICH & SCARFACE. He deported and his brother got hung.

ALI. Ismail.

ISMAIL. Here.

ALI. Abdul.

ABDUL. Here.

ALI. Where's Mohammed Ben Al Kazir?

ARABS. He was caught forging cheques,

SCARFACE & HEINRICH. Got religion and changed his sex.

[MUSIC #17: "THE CUSTOMER'S ALWAYS RIGHT"]

ALI. *(singing)*
WHEN A CRUISE SHIP COMES
I EXPECT YOU BUMS
TO MAKE YOUR OWN DEDUCTIONS
INSPIRED BY GREED
YOU WILL ALL PROCEED
ACCORDING TO INSTRUCTIONS.

ARABS.
THE SUCKERS LAND TODAY
HURRAY, HURRAY, HURRAY!

ALI.
CRINGE, BEG, STEAL, WHINE
NEVER FORGET THE FAMOUS LINE

THE CUSTOMER'S ALWAYS RIGHT MY BOYS
THE CUSTOMER'S ALWAYS RIGHT
THE SON-OF-A-BITCH
IS PROBABLY RICH
SO SMILE WITH ALL YOUR MIGHT
BE WISER THAN A MONKEY
BE ON TO ALL THE TRICKS
IF ONE OF THEM'S A JUNKY
GIVE HIM A BREAK. GIVE HIM A FIX.

ALI.
THE CUSTOMER MAY BE BLACK MY BOYS

OR YELLOW OR BROWN OR WHITE
HE MAY HAVE A YEN FOR RAW RECRUITS
OR MOUNTAIN GOATS OR FOOTBALL BOOTS
BUT SMOOTH HIM
SOOTHE HIM
PANDER TO HIM MORNING NOON AND NIGHT
THE CUSTOMER'S ALWAYS RIGHT.

THE CUSTOMER'S ALWAYS RIGHT MY BOYS
THE CUSTOMER'S ALWAYS RIGHT
THEY MAY PAY A PRICE FOR CURIOUS VICE
OR MERELY WANT A FIGHT
THEY MAY HAVE INHIBITIONS
AND YEARN FOR SECRET JOYS
OBEY YOUR INTUITIONS
OFFER THEM GIRLS…OFFER THEM BOYS
THE CUSTOMER MAY BE DUMB MY BOYS
OR TERRIBLY ERUDITE
PERHAPS YOU CAN SATISFY HIS NEEDS
WITH STRINGS OF RATHER NASTY BEADS
COMPEL HIM
SELL HIM
ANYTHING FROM SEX TO DYNAMITE
REMEMBER BOYS
THE GOD-DAMNED CUSTOMER'S ALWAYS RIGHT,

*(The **ARABS** exit right as **TOURISTS** led by **MIMI** enter from left.)*

MIMI. We now come to the entrance of the famous Kasbah, known since time immemorial as the haunt of sinister and unpredictable characters.

MRS. LUSH. Mrs. Paragon! Tell us the names of some of the characters.

MIMI. Well…there was Haroun Al Raschid…

MRS. LUSH. Yes…

MIMI. And Pepe le Moko…

MRS. LUSH. Pepe le Moko came from Algiers, not Tangiers.

MIMI. Perfectly correct Mrs. Lush, but he used to spend his summers here.

ALVIN. Bang, bang, bang, bang, bang!

MIMI. Don't do that Alvin dear. It interrupts my train of thought. *(reading from book)* It is here, in the scented dusk, that veiled women flit furtively through the twisted cobbled streets, their eyes gleaming like crescent moons above their yashmaks...

ALVIN. I want to ride on a yashmak.

MIMI. People don't ride on yashmaks, Alvin, dear, they wear them, You're probably thinking of a Yak.

ALVIN. What's a yak?

MR. RAWLINGS. Stop yakking

MRS. LUSH. There's no necessity to be rude to the child just because he has an enquiring mind.

MIMI. ...It is at this sacred hour of the day that the Muezzin sounds from the minarets and all good Mohammedans turn their faces towards Mecca in the East and pray to Allah.

MRS. SWEENEY. Mrs. Paragon?

MIMI. Yes, Mrs. Sweeney.

MRS. SWEENEY. What is that white domed building like an inkstand?

MIMI. That's a mosque, Mrs. Sweeney. A mosque is an Arab church. Just like St. Patrick's on Fifth Avenue only you take your shoes off.

ALVIN. Bang, bang, bang, bang.

MIMI. Would you speak to Alvin Mrs. Lush? The dear little chap is driving me mad.

MRS. LUSH. The child's only enjoying himself.

ALVIN. I want a banana split.

MIMI. You'll have to wait until you get back to the ship. They don't make banana splits in Morocco.

ALVIN. What do they make?

MIMI. Leather, Alvin dear, they make great big knotted whips or leather. And now my friends you are at liberty to disperse until three o'clock when I will meet you with the sightseeing bus outside the Grand Hotel and conduct you on a scenic drive of breathtaking fascination. Any gifts or souvenirs you acquire should be deposited at the American Express Office before two forty-five. Stick to mineral water or light wines, lay off fresh salads and don't buy too many carpets. Arrivederci for the momento and God Bless you all.

*(***TOURISTS*** exit right;* **MIMI** *turns and sees* **JOHNNY** *sitting at cafe table.)*

MIMI. Johnny!

JOHNNY. I've been watching your performance. It lacked sincerity.

MIMI. I'll never forgive you.

JOHNNY. You must be worn out. What would you like to drink?

MIMI. A double opium on the rocks.

JOHNNY. You're having lunch with me. Did you know?

MIMI. No I didn't…I…

JOHNNY. I've found out where we can go, There's a beach only a few miles away and we can eat there…on a terrace overlooking the sea.

MIMI. What about your Mother?

JOHNNY. She's going to the British Legation, Sir Gerald and Lady Nutfield are taking her. Mother loves legations and embassies. They feed her sense of importance.

MIMI. Didn't she want you to go too?

JOHNNY. I said I had a headache and the beginnings of a sore throat and so I'd better stay on board. Gin and tonic?

MIMI. Cognac. It's safer.

JOHNNY. One cognac please. That colour suits you. You look wonderful.

MIMI. Thank you. I must cable Bloomingdale's. They need encouragement.

JOHNNY. It's your night off tonight isn't it?

MIMI. Officially yes.

JOHNNY. You're having dinner with me…did you know?

MIMI. No I didn't…I…

JOHNNY. We'll find somewhere quiet.

MIMI. Now see here Johnny…

JOHNNY. Please don't say no. It means a lot to me.

MIMI. Does it Johnny…does it really?

JOHNNY. You know it does.

MIMI. What about your sore throat.

JOHNNY. I'll gargle all afternoon.

MIMI. Johnny. It's strictly against the rules for me to dally, hobnob, or fraternize with any of the passengers… what time?

JOHNNY. Let's meet here at this cafe at say 8:30.

MIMI. Yes.

JOHNNY. Will you be all right here for a few minutes while I go and arrange about the car?

MIMI. Yes.

JOHNNY. And will you deposit your guilty conscience at the American Express office as of now?

MIMI. Yes. To hell with it.

JOHNNY. I adore you,

> (**JOHNNY** *exits.* **ARAB** *down left starts playing flute. Other* **ARABS** *try, to sell* **MIMI** *trinkets. She sits smiling at them.*)

> **[MUSIC #18: "SOMETHING'S VERY STRANGE – NEW"]**

MIMI. *(singing)*
THIS IS NOT A DAY LIKE ANY OTHER DAY
THIS IS SOMETHING SPECIAL AND APART
SOMETHING TO REMEMBER

WHEN THE COLDNESS OF DECEMBER
CHILLS MY HEART.

SOMETHING VERY STRANGE
IS HAPPENING TO ME
EVERY FACE I SEE
SEEMS TO BE SMILING
ALL THE SOUNDS I HEAR
THE BUSES CHANGING GEAR
SUDDENLY APPEAR
TO BE BEGUILING
NOBODY IS MELANCHOLY
NOBODY IS SAD
NOT A SINGLE SHADOW ON THE SEA
SOME MAGICIAN'S SPELL
HAS MADE THIS MAGIC START
AND I FEEL I WANT TO HOLD EACH SHINING MOMENT IN
    MY HEART
SOMETHING STRANGE AND GAY
ON THIS ENCHANTED DAY
SEEMS TO BE
HAPPENING TO ME.

(**ARABS** *crowd around* **MIMI**, *She takes a kerchief from one and gives them all money.*)

SOMETHING VERY STRANGE
IS HAPPENING TO ME
EVERY CAT I SEE
SEEMS TO BE PURRING
I CAN CLEARLY TELL
IN EVERY CLANGING BELL
SOME FORGOTTEN MELODY
RECURRING
TINKER, TAILOR, SOLDIER SAILOR,
BEGGAR-MAN OR THIEF
EVERY SINGLE LEAF
ON EVERY TREE
SEEMS TO BE AWARE
OF SOMETHING IN THE AIR

AND IF ONLY I WERE YOUNGER I'D PUT RIBBONS IN MY HAIR
SOMETHING STRANGE AND GAY
ON THIS ROMANTIC DAY

SEEMS TO BE
HAPPENING TO ME!

(exit)

Scene Two

[MUSIC #19: "NEW TAORMINA"]

(ITALIAN INTERLUDE – BALLET)

(The lights come up on a square in any small town in Sicily, Far away in the background can be seen the Coronia anchored in the harbour.)

*(As the scene begins we find a small group of **ITALIAN VILLAGERS** happily preparing for a festive occasion of some sort. There is a **YOUNG MAN** on a ladder Upstage Right hanging a banner, with 'Buona Fortuna' painted on it, so it spans the street. A **WOMAN** stands below him, next to what looks like a large wooden crate, giving him instructions in her native tongue, A **MAN** is seated Downstage Left reading a current copy of 'Life' magazine and drinking from a bottle of Coca-Cola while another **WOMAN** sings as she kneels on the ground scrubbing some clothes in a large washtub upstage of him. Another **MAN** enters Downstage Right with several six-packs of Ballantine Beer which he proceeds to open and pour with great abandon into a beer keg Upstage Left.)*

*(A **THIRD WOMAN** enters from Upstage Left with a very large tiered wedding cake which she sets down proudly on the wooden crate. A **LITTLE BOY** runs on from Downstage Left, goes to the cake and runs his finger over the icing as the **TWO WOMEN** shoo him off Right with cries of "Basta Basta!" He returns almost immediately shouting excitedly and pointing offstage.)*

*(A NATIVE WEDDING PARTY enters preceded by a **PRIEST** and followed by a **BRIDE** and **GROOM**, a **FLOWER GIRL**, **THREE BRIDESMAIDS** and their **ESCORTS**. The group's arrival causes a great deal of excitement and everyone crowds around the **BRIDE** and **GROOM**, kissing and congratulating them. The **MAN** Downstage Left signals for silence, jumps up on his chair and accompanying himself on a guitar starts singing a mournful rock* 'n' roll version of 'O Bambino.'*)*

(After he has sung a few lines, there is unrestrained applause from everyone on stage and with shouts and laughter a general dance begins, during which a bottle is produced and passed among the **MEN***. The* **BRIDE** *and* **GROOM** *are urged to dance and they perform a short lyric variation for the admiring* **GROUP***. Gradually everyone joins in and the dancing reaches a Wild climax.)*

(Suddenly the **LITTLE BOY** *rushes on from Upstage Left. He gives a short blast on the bugle he is carrying and immediately the dancing stops. Everybody freezes for a moment and then in a frenzy of haste proceeds to prepare themselves for the arrival of the tourists from the Coronia, The* **BRIDE** *hastily strips to her underclothing, the* **LITTLE BOY** *and* **FLOWER GIRL** *are quickly dressed in rags, one of the* **WOMEN** *opens the wooden crate to reveal a stock of neatly arranged souvenirs and postcards, the wedding cake is taken off-stage, the washtub is pushed into place, bunches of grapes are hurriedly flung into it, another* **WOMAN** *brings on two large pizza pies, etc.)*

(As all the **ITALIANS** *get into set positions, the music of 'You're A Long Long Way From America" in march tempo begins and the Coronia* **PASSENGERS***, including the* **CANDIJACKS***, the* **SWEENEYS***,* **MRS. LUSH***, etc., all with cameras poised, march in, neatly in step, from Upstage Right. As a body they turn and gaze wide-eyed at the spectacle in the Square; from the* **MAN** *downstage right with a large sign, 'Original Masterpieces 850 Lire' which he flips over revealing a reproduction of the 'Mona Lisa' to the* **TWO CHILDREN** *in rags sitting on the ground next to him drinking from Chianti bottles, to the* **WOMAN** *Stage Left at the washtub with her sign, 'Crush it Yourself Wine 350 Lire," and finally to the* **BRIDE** *Upstage Centre being serenaded by the* **GROOM** *and looking disheveled and very much the tart as she displays the sign on her back, '200 Lire,' The* **TOURISTS'** *cameras click and flashbulbs pop as the scene blacks out.)*

Scene Three

[MUSIC #19A: "NAPLES INTRO"]

(NAPLES. THE SUN DECK. NIGHT.)

(Downstage Left **MRS. VAN MIER** *and* **MRS. SPENCER BOLLARD** *are seated at a table.* **MRS. SPENCER BOLLARD** *has finished her nightly glass of milk.* **MRS. VAN MIER** *as usual, is working at her embroidery frame.)*

*(***NANCY*** *crosses from Right to Left with* **BARNABY** *laughing and talking.)*

ELINOR. Nancy – Nancy – NANCY!

*(***NANCY*** *pays no attention whatever and she and* **BARNABY** *go off.)*

MRS. MIER. I do hope your niece is proving to be an efficient secretary.

ELINOR. I should be lost without her.

*(***MR. & MRS. SWEENEY*** *come on. They look uncertainly at* **MRS. VAN MIER** *for a moment, and then come up to the table.)*

MRS. SWEENEY. It's been a lovely day hasn't it?

MRS. MIER. *(without looking up)* Lovely.

MRS. SWEENEY. Mr. Sweeney and I drove all the way to Sorrento this afternoon. Didn't we, Edgar?

MR. SWEENEY. Yes sweetheart.

MRS. SWEENEY. *(after a pause)* And then we drove all the way back again.

MRS. MIER. How sensible.

MRS. SWEENEY. Come Edgar. Beddy-byes. Goodnight.

ELINOR. Goodnight.

(They amble off.)

MRS. MIER. I can't think where people like that come from!

ELINOR. A comfortable suburban house with a double garage and a view or the golf course. People Mrs. Van Mier! *(She gives a complacent little laugh.)* People are the absorbing passion of my life. They are also of course my bread and butter. That's why I never allow myself to be bored for an instant.

MRS. MIER. I'm sure you're very fortunate.

(At this moment **MR. RAWLINGS** *and* **MR. CANDIJACK** *stroll across. Both of them are laughing loudly and* **MR. RAWLINGS** *is obviously staggering. They go off.)*

ELINOR. For instance how would you describe those two men?

MRS. MIER. *(looking after them)* Drunk.

ELINOR. *(triumphantly)* Exactly! But why are they drunk?

MRS. MIER. Because they want to be I suppose.

ELINOR. It goes deeper than that, much much deeper. They're psychologically insecure.

MRS. MIER. I still don't see why they should make quite as much noise about it.

ELINOR. Has it ever occurred to you Mrs. Van Mier that every single person travelling on this ship, with the possible exception of myself, is either escaping or pursuing?

MRS. MIER. How do you mean?

ELINOR. Well take the over-exuberant Mimi Paragon for example. Underneath all that professional vivacity it is obvious that she is escaping from something inside herself, some lonely area of discontent.

MRS. MIER. I think I should describe her as pursuing rather than escaping. She certainly seems to be setting her cap at my son.

ELINOR. Aha! That's your Achilles heel Mrs. Van Mier… your son. It sticks out a mile.

MRS. MIER. I don't see how anyone's heel could stick out a mile.

ELINOR. I think, if you don't mind my saying so, that you worry about your son too much.

MRS. MIER. It is my duty as his mother to protect him from undesirable influences. I fear he takes after his poor father as far as women are concerned. Absolutely no discrimination.

ELINOR. He's a grown man. You can't expect to keep him tied to your apron strings indefinitely

MRS. MIER. Being neither a trained nurse nor a housemaid I have no apron strings.

ELINOR. Touche! Touche!

MRS. MIER. I must frankly say Mrs. Spencer-Ballard that I find your flippancy misplaced to say the least. I am profoundly disturbed about my son's infatuation with this creature, and all you do is talk a lot of nonsense about Achilles' heels and aprons strings.

ELINOR. I am not in the habit of talking nonsense. I was merely trying to give a little friendly advice. However, if it is not taken in the spirit in which it was given, I have nothing more to say. Goodnight, Mrs. Van Mier, *(she rises)* I can only hope that you will be in a less disagreeable mood in the morning. "Sudden she rages like the troubled Main…Now sinks the storm and all is calm again!" *(She laughs cheerfully and goes off.)*

*(***MRS. VAN MIER*** looks after her balefully and proceeds to put her embroidery frame away in her work bag. ***MIMI*** and ***JOHNNY*** come on gaily from the right. They are both in evening dress.)*

JOHNNY. Why mother. You should have been in bed hours ago.

(He kisses her.)

MRS. MIER. I shouldn't have been able to sleep dear, not knowing where you were.

JOHNNY. Nonsense dear. I told you I was taking Mimi to the Gala dinner at the Excelsior.

MRS. MIER. I'm sure I hope you enjoyed yourselves.

MIMI. We certainly did. Your son is wonderful company Mrs. Van Mier. Won't you have a nightcap with us?

MRS. MIER. I'm afraid I don't feel quite up to it. I shall ask the stewardess to bring some hot milk to my cabin. Goodnight Johnny

(She kisses him.)

Goodnight Mrs. Paragon. Don't keep my boy up too late.

*(**MRS. VAN MIER** churns off. **MIMI** looks after her a trifle ruefully.)*

MIMI. I did my best but it didn't seem to work too well.

JOHNNY. Oh don't worry about mother. She's only in one of her moods.

MIMI. As far as I'm concerned her mood seems to remain fairly consistent. *(She laughs.)* Thanks for a lovely evening anyway.

JOHNNY. You're not angry are you?

MIMI. Of course not, don't be silly. I'm just tired. I've been up since 8:30 this morning. A carefree personally conducted tour, Thirty-three eager beavers squeezed into five automobiles and a picnic lunch on a hunk of lava. We've been round Vesuvius, up Vesuvius, and down Vesuvius. Dear little Alvin Lush nearly fell into the crater…no no…some spoilsport pulled him back.

JOHNNY. What about that nightcap?

MIMI. I don't think I'd better, Johnny. I really am tired

JOHNNY. Please don't go. Not just yet. You can't leave me alone with all this going on. Just look at those stars and the lights on the sea.

MIMI. Yes, I'm looking.

JOHNNY. I suppose they're fishing boats.

MIMI. Yes. I guess they are.

JOHNNY. And listen to those mandolins playing in the distance.

MIMI. Yes, I'm listening. But the mandolins don't play forever.

JOHNNY. Who cares! They're playing now.

MIMI. I care Johnny. I care about a whole lot of things. Please let me go.

JOHNNY. No, not this time. It's too late.

[MUSIC #20: "DON'T TURN AWAY FROM LOVE"]

MIMI. *(looking at him)* Too late?

JOHNNY. Too late to pretend any longer.

MIMI. *(troubled)* I'm not pretending anything.

JOHNNY. *(urgently)* Yes you are. You're pretending that this – this feeling between us is nothing more than a sort of casual flirtation, just something to be enjoyed lightly, without getting involved, without committing yourself in anyway. But what you're pretending just isn't true. It might have been true at the beginning, but it isn't any more. It's gone beyond that and you know it.

MIMI. Johnny please…

JOHNNY. When I first talked to you I thought you were the most honest woman I'd ever met, but you're not being honest now, either with yourself or with me, if you don't admit that you want me every bit as much as I want you, and it doesn't matter if it lasts for an hour or for a day or for ever, it's true now, at this moment, just as the moon and the stars and the damned mandolins are true. Don't deny it – don't turn away from it – please –

(He sings.)

DON'T TURN AWAY FROM LOVE
BECAUSE YOU KNOW THERE'LL BE AN END TO IT
NO LYRIC LOVER'S SONG
HAS EVER LASTED LONG
WHY NOT BE TENDER TO IT
LET YOUR HEART SURRENDER TO IT
DON'T TURN AWAY FROM LOVE
DON'T PLAY IT FALSE OR CONDESCEND TO IT

HERE IN THE MOONLIGHT WITH THE EAGER STARS
DON'T TURN AWAY FROM LOVE.

DON'T TURN AWAY FROM LOVE
NO MATTER WHAT IT HOLDS IN STORE FOR YOU
DON'T FEAR THE PAIN IT BRINGS
IF ONCE AGAIN IT BRINGS
THAT SWEETNESS EVERY LOVER
IN HIS HEART CAN RE-DISCOVER
DON'T TURN AWAY FROM LOVE
PLEASE LET THE MUSIC PLAY ONCE MORE FOR YOU
HERE IN THE MOONLIGHT WITH THE EAGER STARS ABOVE
DON'T TURN AWAY FROM LOVE
DON'T TURN AWAY FROM LOVE!

(Suddenly **MIMI**, *whose head has been averted, looks at* **JOHNNY** *and surrenders to the pleading in his eyes. She puts her arms round his neck and pulls his mouth down to hers.)*

Scene Four

[MUSIC #20A: "LIFE BOAT INTRO"]

(THE PROMENADE DECK. EVENING.)

(The ship is lying in the bay of Villefranche. **MR. & MRS. SWEENEY** *are sitting at a table, staring silently into space. A party of* **TOURISTS** *come on and pass across the deck, laughing and talking. When they have gone,* **MRS. SWEENEY** *breaks the silence.)*

MRS. SWEENEY. So you just drifted into the Casino while I was having my hair done.

MR. SWEENEY. *(gloomily)* Yes, sweetheart

MRS. SWEENEY. And you just happened to sit down at the Roulette tables?

MR. SWEENEY. Yes, sweetheart,

MRS. SWEENEY. And you just happened to lose seven hundred and ninety-three dollars?

MR. SWEENEY. Yes, sweetheart.

MRS. SWEENEY. And you didn't happen to remember before drifting into the Casino that I had particularly asked you to buy these table mats for Mrs. Teitelbaum, the perfume for Louella and those three printed scarves that I picked out for the Pendleton girls?

MR. SWEENEY. No, sweetheart.

MRS. SWEENEY. I sincerely hope that God may forgive you, Edgar, for I never shall.

(They begin to sing.)

"BRONXVILLE DARBY AND JOAN"

Verse 1.

WE DO NOT FEAR THE VERDICT OF POSTERITY
OUR LIVES HAVE BEEN TOO HUMDRUM AND MUNDANE
IN THE TWILIGHT OF OUR DAYS

MR. & MRS. SWEENEY.

HAVING REACHED THE FINAL PHASE
IN ALL SINCERITY
WE MUST EXPLAIN.

Refrain 1.

WE'RE A DEAR OLD COUPLE AND WE HATE ONE ANOTHER
AND WE'VE HATED ONE ANOTHER FOR A LONG LONG TIME
SINCE THE DAY THAT WE WERE WED, UP TO THE PRESENT
OUR LIVES, WE MUST CONFESS
HAVE BEEN PROGRESSIVELY MORE UNPLEASANT
WE'RE JUST SWEET OLD DARLINGS WHO DESPISE ONE
    ANOTHER
WITH A THOROUGHNESS APPROACHING THE SUBLIME
BUT THROUGH ALL OUR YEARS
WE'VE BEEN AFFECTIONATELY KNOWN
AS THE BRONXVILLE DARBY AND JOAN,

Verse 2.

OUR GOLDEN WEDDING PASSED WITH ALL OUR FAMILY
AN ORGY OF REMEMBRANCE AND RUE
IN ACKNOWLEDGEMENT OF THIS
WE EXCHANGED A LOVING KISS
A TRIFLE CLAMMILY
BECAUSE WE KNEW.

Refrain 2

WE'RE A DEAR OLD COUPLE WHO DETEST ONE ANOTHER
WE'VE DETESTED ONE ANOTHER SINCE OUR BRIDAL NIGHT
WHICH WAS SQUALID, UNATTRACTIVE AND CONVULSIVE
AND PROVED, BEYOND DISPUTE
THAT WE WERE MUTUALLY REPULSIVE
WE'RE JUST SWEET OLD DARLINGS WHO TORMENT ONE
    ANOTHER
WITH THE UTMOST MALICIOUSNESS AND SPITE
AND THROUGH ALL OUR YEARS
WE'VE BEEN INACCURATELY KNOWN
AS THE BRONXVILLE DARBY AND JOAN,

(They exit and re-enter for Refrain 3.)

Refrain 3.

WE'RE A DEAR OLD COUPLE AND WE LOATHE ONE
    ANOTHER
WITH A LOATHING THAT ENGULFS US LIKE A TIDAL WAVE
WITH OUR DEEP SUB-CONSCIOUS MINDS WE SELDOM
    DABBLE
BUT SOMETHING MUST IMPEL
THE WORDS WE SPELL
WHEN WE'RE PLAYING "SCRABBLE"
WE 1 RE JUST SWEET OLD DARLINGS WHO ABHOR ONE
    ANOTHER
AND WE'LL BORE EACH OTHER FIRMLY TO THE GRAVE
BUT THROUGH ALL OUR YEARS WE'VE BEEN REFERRED TO
    MORE OR LESS
AS THE BRONXVILLE PORGY AND BESS.

Scene Five

(THE PARTHENON – ATHENS)

(When the lights fade in on the scene, **ELINOR SPENCER-BOLLARD** *is pacing back and forth dictating to* **NANCY** *who is seated on the ground with a notebook in her lap.)*

ELINOR. Chapter Twenty-two, page 280, Tracy sprang at Sylvia with a snarl, Sylvia shrank back cowering against the Tudor paneling, her hands stretched out supplicatingly before her...

NANCY. How do you spell supplicatingly?

ELINOR. I neither know nor care, "Then, in a voice shaken with sobs, she whispered, 'For the love of heaven don't shoot, I am carrying your child.'" That's good, that's very good, "Tracy turned on his heel and with a muttered imprecation, stumbled from the room."

NANCY. How do you spell imprecation?

ELINOR. The usual way. Really Nancy you must not keep interrupting.

NANCY. I'm sorry Aunt Elinor.

ELINOR. Where was I?

NANCY. With a muttered what-do-you-call-it he stumbled from the room.

ELINOR. "Whimpering like a stricken animal Sylvia slithered to the floor unconscious." That's lovely! Now let me see those notes.

NANCY. You wouldn't understand them. They're in shorthand.

ELINOR. There's nothing written down here at all.

NANCY. Isn't there? I could have sworn there was. There must be something wrong with my pencil. It's a dear little green pencil. I bought it when we came ashore.

ELINOR. Dear little green grandmother.

NANCY. A friend of mine has a dear little Greek grandmother. Her name is Mrs. Popalopolis. Mrs. Popalopolis,

ELINOR. Have you gone mad?

NANCY. Yes, Aunt Elinor.

ELINOR. You haven't taken down one word I've been dictating to you for the last hour.

NANCY. Not a word.

ELINOR. I think you'd better go back to the ship and lie down.

NANCY. I don't want to lie down. I want to fly through the air like a bird.

ELINOR. Nancy. Pull yourself together!

NANCY. Aunt Elinor, I've fallen in love.

ELINOR. I was afraid this would happen.

NANCY. I was afraid it wouldn't. His name's Barnaby.

ELINOR. I gathered that from your vocal outbursts, What does he do?

NANCY. He's going to be an architect or an agriculturalist. I forget which. I know it starts with an 'A.'

ELINOR. Has anything happened between you that shouldn't have happened?

NANCY. No it hasn't…not yet.

ELINOR. Well see that it doesn't dear.

NANCY. I've let you down, haven't I?

ELINOR. Help me up.

NANCY. Aunt Elinor, you won't send me home in disgrace, will you?

ELINOR. Certainly not. It would be far too expensive.

NANCY. What are you going to do?

ELINOR. What I should have done in the first place. Buy a Dictaphone.

NANCY. Aunt Elinor.

ELINOR. What is it?

NANCY. I love you very much!

ELINOR. Youth. Youth – In gallant trim the gilded vessel goes. Youth at the prow, and Pleasure at the helm, Heigh Ho!

(ELINOR exits right. NANCY hides behind upstage column as MIMI and JOHNNY enter from left.)

MIMI. I don't suppose anyone has came up those damned steps so fast since the Spartans in B.C. whatever it was.

JOHNNY. You've got to say yes.

MIMI. How can I say yes? I've got to get all those tourists through all those ruins and back to the ship.

JOHNNY. I'll be waiting for you in the lobby of the hotel from eight-thirty on, We'll have a little dinner and come up here afterwards in the moonlight.

MIMI. I don't think my feet could stand it.

JOHNNY. I'll carry you.

MIMI. I don't think your feet could stand it.

(JOHNNY picks her up.)

Put me down! They'll be here in a minute, I can hear them coming.

JOHNNY. You've got to say yes.

MIMI. All right. I'll be there. I should have my head examined but I'll be there.

(JOHNNY puts MIMI down and as he exits right, MRS. LUSH followed by the TOURISTS enters from left.)

MRS. LUSH. Ah, there you are Mrs. Paragon. We didn't know which way you were going.

MIMI. I'm a bit confused about that myself. And this, my friends, is the most spectacular, the most sensational, the most famous ruin in the whole wide world. The Parthenon.

ELMER. Whoever built it must have had a good look at the Pennsylvania Station.

MAIMIE. Elmer!

ALVIN. I'm a train! I'm a train! I'm a great big train! Whoo, whoo, whoo…

MIMI. Mrs. Lush, do you think you could persuade Alvin to be a great big train a little further off?

MRS. LUSH. The child's only enjoying himself. He's naturally high spirited.

MIMI. We are all aware of that, Mrs. Lush. He has been oppressively high spirited ever since we left Staten Island.

ALVIN. Whoo, whoo, whoo, whoo...

MAIMIE. Perhaps it would have been better to have left him on board, Mrs. Lush. He is a little young to go sightseeing.

MRS. LUSH. I brought my son on this trip to see Europe, Mrs. Candijack, and Europe is what he is going to see.

MIMI. The name Parthenon, generally accepted since the Fourth Century B.C., was originally associated with the cult of Athena Parthenos, the virgin...

ELMER. Cult of the virgin? Your brother Fred sure would have appreciated this.

MAIMIE. Will you lay off my brother Fred, Elmer. You're always making snide' cracks about him. It was as much her fault as his anyway.

MIMI. Mr. and Mrs. Candijack, whoever's fault whoever that was, could I have your undivided attention for just a few minutes. It was in the Fourth Century B.C...

ALVIN. What's a virgin, Momma?

MRS. LUSH. You'll find out when you're older dear.

MR. RAWLINGS. And when you do, you send me a postal card with the name and address.

MAIMIE. For shame, Mr. Rawlings. In front of an innocent child!

ALVIN. I want to know what a virgin is...l want to know what a virgin is...

MIMI. A virgin, Alvin, is a lady who has not been married. And if your mother had not been married you would not have been on this cruise, and if you had not been on this cruise, I for one would not be on the verge of a nervous breakdown.

MRS. LUSH. I resent your attitude to Alvin, Mrs. Paragon. You're always picking on him.

MIMI. The time has come, MRS. Lush, for me to cast discretion to the winds and give you a teensy weensy morceau of unvarnished truth. I hate Alvin.

MRS. LUSH. How dare you say such things, I'll complain to the Captain.

MIMI. I think it only fair to warn you that the Captain hates Alvin too. In fact I cannot off-hand think of one single living creature on the ship who doesn't long to kick the merry little fellow's teeth down his merry little throat.

MRS. LUSH. Mrs. Paragon…

MIMI. He is a precocious, ill-mannered, noisy, spoilt little monster, and I warn you here and now that if you go on encouraging him to make a rude, undisciplined little pig of himself, a day will dawn when he will bring your orange hair in sorrow to the grave.

MR. RAWLINGS. Hear! Hear!

MRS. LUSH. I'll report you for this. I'll have you thrown off the ship!

MIMI. You'd be doing me a favour.

MRS. LUSH. Come on, honey, you and mother will go back on board and have ourselves a lovely chocolate malted.

ALVIN. I don't want a chocolate malted, I want a banana split.

MRS. LUSH. You will have what I tell you to have so shut up!

(**MRS. LUSH** *and* **ALVIN** *exit left.*)

ELMER. You're a courageous woman, Mrs. Paragon, and I'd like to shake you by the hand.

MIMI. I appreciate the thought Mr. Candijack but we have no time to waste. I've got to tell you all about Ancient Greece before dinner and it's nearly seven o'clock now. As Helen of Troy said when she first saw that old wooden horse…Avanti Garibaldi!

*(**MIMI** leads the **TOURISTS** off right, **BARNABY** stays behind. **NANCY** comes from behind column.)*

NANCY. Barnaby…!

BARNABY. Oh. You made me jump.

NANCY. I was just behind the pillar.

BARNABY. I've been looking all over for you for two hours.

NANCY. Have you?

BARNABY. Where's your Aunt gone?

NANCY. To buy a dictaphone.

BARNABY. You look wonderful against all this. Hold still for a minute.

NANCY. For the love of Heaven don't shoot, I am carrying your child.

BARNABY. You've gone out of your mind.

NANCY. Whimpering like a stricken animal she cowered back against the Tudor paneling.

BARNABY. What are you talking about?

NANCY. Tudor paneling. You ought to know all about that. You're going to be an architect.

BARNABY. I'm not. I'm going to be an archeologist.

NANCY. I knew it started with an 'A.'

[MUSIC #21: "WHEN YOU WANT ME"]

BARNABY. *(singing)*
I'LL HAVE TO GET THE BEES AND BIRDS TO TELL YOU
THAT I'VE LOVED YOU FROM THE START
I SIMPLY HAVEN'T GOT THE WORDS TO TELL YOU
WHAT IS TRULY IN MY HEART
JOKING APART.

WHEN YOU WANT ME – IF YOU WANT ME
CALL ME – CALL ME – IF YOU CARE.

NANCY.
LISTEN IT'S SO FUNNY YOU MENTION IT, I WAS JUST.

BARNABY.
WHEN YOU NEED ME – IF YOU NEED ME
SAY SO – SAY SO – I'LL BE THERE

NANCY.

LISTEN I'M SAYING SO…

BARNABY.

I'VE NOTHING BUT MY HEART TO BRING YOU
NO MONEY BUT A QUESTING MIND
BUT IF THIS LITTLE SONG I SING TO YOU
MEANS A THING TO YOU
PLEASE BE KIND.

NANCY.

WELL, NOW THAT YOU'VE ASKED ME…

BARNABY.

WHEN YOU'RE LONELY – IF YOU'RE LONELY
CALL ME – CALL ME – ANYHOW.

NANCY.

I DON'T THINK I'D REACH YOU, BARNABY!

BARNABY.

IF YOU WANT ME – NEED ME – LOVE ME

BARNABY.	**NANCY.**
TELL ME	UH HUH
TELL ME	YES!

BARNABY.

TELL ME NOW!

NANCY.

I'LL LOVE YOU LONGER THAN 'THE FORSYTE SAGA'
AND I'LL TREMBLE AT YOUR FROWN

BARNABY.

I'D LIKE TO CABLE TO BALENCIAGA
TO PREPARE YOUR WEDDING GOWN
DON'T LET ME DOWN

NANCY.	BARNABY.
WHEN YOU	WHEN YOU
WANT ME	WANT ME
IF YOU	IF YOU
WANT ME	WANT ME
CALL ME	CALL ME
CALL ME	CALL ME

NANCY & BARNABY.

IF YOU CARE

BARNABY.

I'VE GOT AN ANSWER SERVICE

BARNABY.	NANCY.
WHEN YOU	WHEN YOU
NEED ME	NEED ME
IF YOU	IF YOU
NEED ME	NEED ME
SAY SO	SAY SO
SAY SO	SAY SO

NANCY & BARNABY.

I'LL BE THERE.

NANCY.

I WANT TO MAKE MY FEELINGS CLEAR TO YOU

I'VE NEVER FELT LIKE THIS BEFORE

BARNABY.

I'D SACRIFICE MY WHOLE CAREER TO YOU

TO BE NEAR TO YOU

EVERMORE

NANCY & BARNABY.

WHEN YOU'RE LONELY – IF YOU'RE LONELY

CALL ME – CALL ME – ANYHOW

NANCY.

YOU CAN REVERSE THE CHARGES

NANCY & BARNABY.

IF YOU WANT ME – NEED ME – LOVE ME

TELL ME – TELL ME – HERE AND NOW!

(dance)

BARNABY.

> I REALLY HAVEN'T ANY GOODS AND CHATTELS
> BUT A BEAT-UP CHEVROLET

NANCY.

> I ONLY KNOW I'VE GOT A HEART THAT RATTLES
> EVERY TIME YOU LOOK MY WAY

NANCY & BARNABY.

> THERE'S REALLY NOTHING MORE TO SAY
> EXCEPT THAT I SHOULD LIKE TO STAY
> WITH YOU FOREVER AND A DAY.
> OLE!

Scene Six

[MUSIC #21A: "SAIL AWAY – SOFT"]

(THE SUN DECK – THE EMPTY BAR AT NIGHT)

*(**MIMI** and **JOHNNY** are seated at a table in front of the bar.)*

MIMI. That's the Nantucket light flashing over there. We're getting near home.

JOHNNY. Yes. We're getting near home.

MIMI. I always find the last night of a cruise depressing, A sort of anti-climax…something not quite over and something not quite beginning.

JOHNNY. There's no need to make conversation. I know where I stand. You've made it quite clear.

MIMI. Oh, Johnny, please don't talk like that.

JOHNNY. How do you expect me to talk, It's not very pleasant to be told you're not wanted.

MIMI. Not wanted…I never said you weren't wanted. Okay…to hell with it…there's no sense in trying to explain something to somebody if they won't even listen.

JOHNNY. You don't believe I love you enough do you?

MIMI. Yes, I believe you think you do. That's why I want it to stay as it is. Something we can always remember gratefully, a love affair that didn't die, Come on Johnny let's say goodbye to it now, before it's too late, before everything's spoiled.

JOHNNY. Why are you so certain that everything would be spoiled?

MIMI. Because it just wouldn't work. You have your life and I have mine and they couldn't be further apart. You must know that in your heart as well as I do. Let's face it Johnny, all holidays come to an end.

JOHNNY. Is that all this has meant to you? A holiday?

MIMI. What this has meant to me…what this still means to me, is something I have to figure out for myself.

JOHNNY. What about what it means to me?

MIMI. Every man for himself. Abandon Ship!

JOHNNY. I suppose that's meant to be funny?

MIMI. Maybe. I don't know. It's all a question of point of view, isn't it?

JOHNNY. Mimi…

MIMI. Please let's not argue about this any more, Johnny. We're not getting anywhere.

JOHNNY. If that's the way you feel there's nothing more to be said is there?

MIMI. No there's nothing more to be said

JOHNNY. Goodbye Mimi. *(He exits right.)*

MIMI. Goodbye Johnny.

[MUSIC #22: "LATER THAN SPRING"]

(singing)

I CAN ORGANIZE A TREASURE HUNT
OR EVEN CLOCKWORK TRAINS
ANYTHING…

LATER THAN SPRING
MUCH DISILLUSION COMES
SOMETIMES CONFUSION COMES
YOU LOSE YOUR WAY

NEED IT BE SUCH UNBEARABLE SADNESS
TO FACE THE TRUTH?
LOVE, WITH ITS PASSIONATE MADNESS
BELONGS TO YOUTH.

LATER THAN SPRING
OUR VALUES CHANGE MY DEAR
IT WOULD BE STRANGE MY DEAR
IF THEY SHOULD STAY
WASTE NO TEARS

ON THE HURRYING YEARS
FOR WHATEVER THEY MAY BRING
SONG BIRDS STILL SING
LATER THAN SPRING,

Front Cloth

*(***MRS. VAN MIER*** *crosses Stage with* **STEWARD**.*)*

(Enter **JOEY** *and* **JOE**.*)*

JOHNNY. Joe – it's been a wonderful trip. Thanks for everything.

(They shake hands.)

JOE. You're not going ashore before Mimi's farewell get-together cocktail party?

JOHNNY. I'm afraid so. Mother's got a plane to catch. Joe – be a pal and tell Mimi…No, never mind. Forget it. It doesn't matter.

Scene Seven

(THE SUN DECK. NEW YORK.)

(The ship has docked.)

(The orchestra begins playing the reprise to 'When You Want Me.' On stage are the Coronia's **STAFF** *and most of the* **PASSENGERS**. *During the number they all exchange addresses on small slips of paper. Toward the end of the number the slips are torn into little pieces and scattered like confetti and the* **PASSENGERS** *leave in the following order:* **MR. & MRS. SWEENEY**, **SIR GERARD** *and* **LADY NUTFIELD**, **ELINOR SPENCER-BOLLARD**, **BARNABY** *and* **NANCY**, *the* **CANDIJACK FAMILY**, **MRS. LUSH** *and* **ALVIN**, *and finally,* **JOHNNY** *and* **MRS. VAN MIER**.*)*

(At the end of the 'When You Want Me' reprise, the orchestra plays 'Sail Away' as the **TWO STEWARDS** *cross with Mimi's luggage, her plant, and her balloons.)*

*(***MIMI** *appears Stage Left with Adlai in her arms. She walks on and sits on the step Stage Centre, looking very much alone.)*

*(***JOHNNY** *appears after a moment from the gangway. He crosses to* **MIMI** *who is startled to see him. He quickly takes Adlai from* **MIMI**, *pulls her to her feet, and rushes her off the ship as the orchestra play the last strains of 'Sail Away.')*

PAT, NANCY & ANN.
WHEN YOU WANT ME
PHONE ME, PHONE ME
ANN.
MU SIX TWO
NINE FOUR THREE
RAWLINGS.
WE'LL HAVE A DRINK OR SOMETHING.
CANDIJACKS.

IF I'M NOT IN
TRY ALGONQUIN
FOUR THREE THOUSAND
WHEN YOU'RE FREE

MRS. LUSH.

ALL SATURDAYS ARE QUITE ALL RIGHT WITH US.

ELINOR.

DROP BY AND SEE MY BULLDOG PUP.

ALL.

MAYBE YOU'LL STOP AND HAVE A BITE WITH US
SPEND THE NIGHT WITH US
JUST CALL UP.

NANCY.

DIAL TE TWO
FOUR ONE THREE TWO
THAT WILL GET US
UP TO TEN

BARNABY.

YOU MUST COME TO THE WEDDING

ALVIN.

TRY FILMORE TWO
SIX FIVE FOUR TWO

ALL.

THAT WILL FIND ME
UP TO NOON.

ALVIN.

IF NOT JUST LEAVE A MESSAGE

ALL.

IT'S BEEN SWELL PAL
GIVE A YELL PAL!
WHAT THE HELL PAL
SEE YOU SOON!

(*General exit which leaves* **MIMI** *alone on stage.*)

[MUSIC #23: "WHY DO THE WRONG PEOPLE TRAVEL?"]

MIMI. (*singing*)

TRAVEL THEY SAY IMPROVES THE MIND
AN IRRITATING PLATITUDE
WHICH FRANKLY, ENTRE NOUS
IS VERY FAR FROM TRUE
PERSONALLY I'VE YET TO FIND
THAT LONGITUDE AND LATITUDE
CAN EDUCATE THOSE SCORES
OF MONUMENTAL BORES

WHO TRAVEL IN GROUPS AND HERDS AND TROUPES
OF VARIOUS BREEDS AND SEXES
TILL THE WHOLE WORLD REELS
TO SHOUTS AND SQUEALS
AND THE CLICKING OF ROLLIFLEXES.

WHY DO THE WRONG PEOPLE TRAVEL, TRAVEL, TRAVEL
WHEN THE RIGHT PEOPLE STAY BACK HOME?
WHAT COMPULSION COMPELS THEM
AND WHO THE HELL TELLS THEM
TO DRAG THEIR CANS TO ZANZIBAR
INSTEAD OF STAYING QUIETLY IN OMAHA?
THE TAJ MAHAL
AND THE GRAND CANAL
AND THE SUNNY FRENCH RIVIERA
WOULD BE LESS OPPRESSED
IF THE MIDDLE WEST
WOULD SETTLE FOR SOMEWHERE RATHER NEARER
PLEASE DO NOT THINK THAT I CRITICIZE OR CAVI
AT A GENUINE URGE TO ROAM
BUT WHY OH WHY DO THE WRONG PEOPLE TRAVEL
WHEN THE RIGHT PEOPLE STAY BACK HOME
AND MIND THEIR BUSINESS
WHEN THE RIGHT PEOPLE STAY BACK HOME
WITH CINERAMA
WHEN THE RIGHT PEOPLE STAY BACK HOME
I'M MERELY ASKING
WHY THE RIGHT PEOPLE STAY BACK HOME?

JUST WHEN YOU THINK ROMANCE IS RIPE
IT RATHER SHARPLY DAWNS ON YOU
THAT EACH SWEET SERENADE
IS FOR THE TOURIST TRADE
ANY ATTRACTIVE NATIVE TYPE
WHO RESOLUTELY FAWNS ON YOU
WILL GIVE AS HIS ADDRESS
AMERICAN EXPRESS
THERE ISN'T A ROCK
BETWEEN BANGKOK
AND THE BEACHES OF HISPANIOLA
THAT DOES NOT RECOIL
FROM SUNTAN OIL
AND THE GURGLE OF COCA COLA.

WHY DO THE WRONG PEOPLE TRAVEL, TRAVEL, TRAVEL
WHEN THE RIGHT PEOPLE STAY BACK HOME?
WHAT EXPLAINS THIS MASS MANIA
TO LEAVE PENNSYLVANIA
AND CLACK AROUND LIKE FLOCKS OF GEESE
DEMANDING DRY MARTINIS ON THE ISLES OF GREECE?
IN THE SMALLEST STREET
WHERE THE GOURMETS MEET
THEY INVARIABLY FETCH UP
AND IT'S HARD TO MAKE
THEM ACCEPT A STEAK
THAT ISN'T SERVED RARE AND SMEARED WITH KETCHUP
MILLIONS OF TOURISTS ARE CHURNING UP THE GRAVEL
WHILE THEY GAZE AT ST. PETER'S DOME
BUT WHY OH WHY DO THE WRONG PEOPLE TRAVEL
WHEN THE RIGHT PEOPLE STAY BACK HOME?
AND EAT HOT DOUGHNUTS
WHEN THE RIGHT PEOPLE STAY BACK HOME
WITH ALL THOSE BENEFITS
WHEN THE RIGHT PEOPLE STAY BACK HOME
I SOMETIMES WONDER
WHY THE RIGHT PEOPLE STAY BACK HOME!

WHAT PECULIAR OBSESSIONS
INSPIRE THOSE PROCESSIONS
OF FAMILIES FROM HOUSTON TEX
WITH ALL THOSE CAMERAS AROUND THEIR NECKS
THEY WILL TAKE A TRAIN
OR AN AEROPLANE
FOR AN HOUR ON THE COSTA BRAVA
AND THEY'LL SEE POMPEII
ON THE ONLY DAY
THAT IT'S UP TO ITS ASS IN MOLTEN LAVA
IT WOULD TAKE YEARS TO UNRAVEL – RAVEL – RAVEL
EVERY IMPULSE THAT MAKES THEM ROAM
BUT WHY OH WHY DO THE WRONG PEOPLE TRAVEL
WHEN THE RIGHT PEOPLE STAY BACK HOME
WITH ALL THAT KLEENEX
WHEN THE RIGHT PEOPLE STAY BACK HOME
WITH DR. BROTHERS
WHEN THE RIGHT PEOPLE STAY BACK HOME
WITH ALL THOSE KENNEDYS
WON'T SOMEONE TELL ME
WHY THE RIGHT
I SAY THE RIGHT PEOPLE STAY BACK HOME!

(She exits off right, re-enters by door of cabin and puts her hat and jacket on. **JOHNNY** *enters the cabin. He picks up her suitcase and motions her to pick up plant, doll and handbag. As they leave* **MIMI** *remembers Adlai in the drawer and takes him out. They go of through cabin door, and down gang plank. At the foot or the gangplank he turns her round and kisses her as –)*

(The curtain falls.)

[MUSIC #24: "FINALE ULTIMO"]

www.ingramcontent.com/pod-product-compliance
Lightning Source LLC
Chambersburg PA
CBHW070633120726
47909CB00004B/1417